PRAISE FOR *THE LEGEND OF BARAFFO*

"*The Legend of Baraffo* is a lucid dream of a novel, a fable
fierce in its moral clarity and gorgeous at the line level.
In the town of Baraffo, Moez Surani has created a place so
rich in sensory detail, so wonderfully alive, as to be
unforgettable. There is so much here about the nuances
of longing and belonging, of intimacy and subjugation,
all of it crafted from the simplest human connections—a
conversation, a shared meal, a card game. This is a beautiful
book, written by a bright new literary talent."
OMAR EL AKKAD, SCOTIABANK GILLER PRIZE–WINNING
AUTHOR OF *What Strange Paradise*

"Moez Surani's *The Legend of Baraffo* is about revolution
and love, political will and will not, hunger striking,
friendship, and tender romance. It's about imprisonment,
charisma and wit, wordplay and poetry, and the unrelenting
search for what is just. Babello, a political prisoner,
and Mazzu, an orphan training to be Mayor, are as vivid
as any two characters you are ever going to meet. They are
indelible and deep and burn bright. This novel is like
a lamp underground—it's absolutely brilliant."
LISA MOORE, AUTHOR OF *THIS IS HOW WE LOVE*

"Seamlessly pivoting from fairy tale to one of caution, Surani's novel is a sly exploration of power and all that's crushed to maintain it. His language is hypnotic and lush from beginning to end."
MONIQUE TRUONG, AUTHOR OF *The Sweetest Fruits*

PRAISE FOR
ARE THE RIVERS IN YOUR POEMS REAL

"A mesmerizing, beautiful book."
JORDAN ABEL, GRIFFIN POETRY PRIZE–WINNING
AUTHOR OF *INJUN* AND *NISHGA*

"There's an urgency and immediacy to Moez Surani's fourth collection of poems, in which he grapples with the relationship of poetry and its abstractions to reality."
TORONTO STAR

"Moez Surani is an explorer. *Are the Rivers in Your Poems Real* obsessively catalogues these explorations in an attempt to preserve our world, both personal and political, in its complexity."

PRAISE FOR *OPERATIONS*

"Moez Surani has written a new kind of elegy."

"An incantatory feat."

"An unnerving, frightening book that calls for expansive and paratextual reading."

THE LEGEND OF BARAFFO

MOEZ SURANI

BOOK★HUG PRESS
Toronto 2023

Library and Archives Canada Cataloguing in Publication

Title: The legend of Baraffo : a novel / Moez Surani.
Names: Surani, Moez, 1979– author.
Identifiers: Canadiana (print) 20230223354 | Canadiana (ebook) 20230223362 | ISBN 9781771668415 (softcover) | ISBN 9781771668422 (EPUB) | ISBN 9781771668439 (PDF)
Classification: LCC PS8637.U74 L44 2023 | DDC C813/.6—DC23

The production of this book was made possible through the generous assistance of the Canada Council for the Arts and the Ontario Arts Council. Book*hug Press also acknowledges the support of the Government of Canada through the Canada Book Fund and the Government of Ontario through the Ontario Book Publishing Tax Credit and the Ontario Book Fund.

Book*hug Press acknowledges that the land on which we operate is the traditional territory of many nations, including the Mississaugas of the Credit, the Anishnabeg, the Chippewa, the Haudenosaunee, and the Wendat peoples. We recognize the enduring presence of many diverse First Nations, Inuit, and Métis peoples and are grateful for the opportunity to meet and work on this territory.

For Zara and Laiq,
should they find this worthy.

PROLOGUE

There is, of course, the legend of Baraffo with which we are all familiar. That day, hundreds of years ago, when Isabella accepted a proposal, causing a generation of men to throw themselves from bridges, second-storey windows, and rooftops. So many men lined up to jump from the mayor's roof that they had to wait hours, trading jokes and gossip, for the honour of dying before her. The pile of dead suitors mounted so high that those who were late in lining up had to step carefully from the roof onto the stack of bodies, then jump to their death. Their bodies angled down from the mayor's hilltop home—a crude staircase of affection.

It is said they met in a garden, Isabella seated on the fountain's ledge with a sheet of water behind her, and that after this meeting his love rainbowed to her over the distances of banishment and exile. But such exaggerations are often history's flourishes. The truth is buried below layers of exuberant storytelling, competing reports from the rival newspapers, and Baraffo's buoyant habit of forgetting. Averse to anything that suppresses their spirits, the people of Baraffo deny sombre thoughts, recollecting instead what is jubilant, beautiful, or readily useful. Through this forgetting, the truths of Isabella's adoration, engagement, and illness, are dormant beneath the years of speculation and retellings that weave into a generalized, piecemeal fable.

The people of Baraffo often pause in the tumult of their unlikely lives and consider that couple's example, and from time to time the people of the town swing their arms out wide to show the magnitude of Isabella's beauty. "This much," they cry.

Their lives blossom in the shade of their people's epic.

In Isabella's Square, at the centre of Baraffo, water rises through a spring-fed fountain, falls in a mist off the top tier, collects in a middle bowl, and becomes mist again in its final descent. The crucial scenes of her life are inscribed in the stone.

A woman sits on the fountain's ledge, the curtain of water behind her while the man waves his arms, the camera that hangs from his neck banging against his chest as he tries to part the crowds and catch his beloved in a dignified pose.

When a new mayor took office a generation or two ago, he declared the first day of summer a holiday to commemorate Isabella's engagement. He ordered sofas, pillows, carpets, and mattresses be pushed below windows so the town's bachelors could safely display their honour by jumping from their roofs and windows. After this proof of gallantry, the streets fill with music and food and everyone drinks through the summer's first week. The town having become a giant living room, people pass out on some mattress or cushion, only to wake later, rub their faces and rejoin the festivity. By declaring this anniversary a holiday, that mayor flipped tragedy into celebration and pushed Baraffo's reputation for extravagance beyond its natural borders—the sea to the east and the mountains to the west.

§

Unable to sleep, a girl steps barefoot from her bed and rewinds her music box. The tune clinks out, the couple on top of her music box turning together in a rigid dance. She climbs back into bed as the hollow tune clinks and sings and that legendary couple, moved by hidden gears and devices, turn together in the darkness of her room.

PART 1

1

In the morning, the smell of roasted coffee roams the streets of Baraffo. The coffee merchants, situated at strategic intersections, ladle out helpings. Some of them discuss politics, others rumours or theological paradoxes. As long as the talk intrigues, people stay and drink more helpings. The coffee stand nearest the coast is dominated by talk of Zuraffi, the poet who was rising in influence throughout the town, the poet who had filled her pages and taken her expression to the streets, writing on stones or a leaf, a shell of a ravaged melon, along a fence, down the length of a stranger's arm, the ink tumbling through pores. The inscribed stones pass between people's hands and the leaves are plucked from the wind and shelved back into a subsequent gust. Sipping coffee, one dedicated merchant gestures directions and whispers what he knows about the whereabouts of the poet's latest offering. His customers converge upon the fragments. They debate their likely sequence and argue over merit and sincerity. Some copy the verse onto their hands or a leg of their pants so they can reread it later.

Zuraffi was writing before Papa became mayor—before Papa, the plump, dark-haired woman whose monumental term of office sprawled across generations, became known by the people of the town as Papa. Even at the outset of her lengthy term, Papa gave the impression that she bathed in some separate, exquisite water. With her diplomacy and warmth, she ran uncontested. Term after term, even with the town's unorthodox open-election procedure, she was marked down as Baraffo's sole candidate.

As she aged, and as her habits and tastes altered, one unchanged aspect of Papa's routine was her afternoon walks, which later mayors would emulate. On these walks, she consumed innumerable glasses of juice, tea, and water, and pried into all the town's happenings: the rivalries and complaints, recipes, ambitions, dissent, the wagers, the novel chess openings, the favoured games of the town's infants, variations in mores and health and remedies, all of the previous night's quarrels, as well as the daily confessions of sin, irritability, and love. The mayor listened to these outpourings with equanimity, nodding while townspeople spoke, with her hands clasped over her stomach while her thumbs circled one another. Papa was emotional about all matters of the town, but strictly rational in her personal affairs. Her great leap occurred late in her life when, with her long hair white and braided back, she adopted a boy whose parents had died in a fire. "I have an empty room," Papa simply said, after so many years of living alone. Because of the mayor's nature, which made her cagey when she was asked about things closest to her heart, Papa never confessed to the softness she felt for the inquiring boy she would meet in the midst of her walks.

§

In the darkness, the boy stands on the sloped roof of his best friend's house. Mazzu rolls his shirtsleeve up and begins windmilling his arm. Wind blows against his shirt and the leaves above. "Vullie, you are my best friend, but I will hit you if you don't come to help me tonight. I don't want to; you are like a brother to me, but I will."

"Come, Mazzu, you don't want to hit me. I am twice your size."

"But I'm wild, Vullie! I'm wild like a monkey! You won't even see it coming. You'll remember tomorrow, though. You'll wake tomorrow and remember that Mazzu, wild like a monkey, had hit you."

Vullie leans over his meal. Rows of houses stretch before him, and Zuraffi's red-brick tower rises to his left. Far ahead of him, the mayor's home sits atop a bluff and overlooks the town. He can discern the sea only as a darkness in the distance. "No, Mazzu, you don't want to hit me. I may hit back."

"I'll remember this. I'll remember who it was that would rather eat second dinner than help their lifelong friend."

"Forget about Giulietta. You've visited her the last four nights. Each night we carried the ladder across town. Each night you climbed to her room, and each night you gave her a fruit I would have gladly eaten. And for what?"

"Very well, then. If this is the way you feel, what I'll do is learn to walk on stilts. Then I'll be able to bring her a mango each day—as I have promised—without the help of my best friend. People will see my shadow cross the moon. 'There goes

Mazzu the stilt walker,' they will say. Each night I'll strap a mango to my head and walk to her house. I'll walk on my stilts above the lights of windows, above the trees, to deliver her my fruit. But remember this, Vullie, when I am mayor one day, as Papa is training me for—"

"Come, let's go," Vullie says, setting aside the empty plate.

They walk to the edge of the roof with Mazzu's arm around Vullie's shoulder. "You know what the people will all say? They will say, 'There goes Vullie, the man so tall his friend had no need for stilts!'"

The two boys step into the arms of a tree. They climb through the branches and thump into the grass. With a ladder under their right arms and Vullie yelling their way through crowds, they march to Giulietta's.

§

Behind Giulietta's home, Vullie braces the ladder that angles all the way to her window. High atop the rungs, Mazzu taps on the window. He waits for her to turn then pulls her bedroom window open. "Giulietta, you grow more beautiful every day. You know, even if your lips were lemons and your tongue like a pickle, still I would cross town to bring you a mango," he says, pulling the gift from his bag.

"Mazzu, even if I had a sailor's portion of wine and you had muscles of an entire army, still I would cross oceans to escape you."

Stretching from the window, Mazzu sets the fruit on her desk. It rolls over onto its side. "You know, I was thinking of you today. I was thinking of our great luck: to have found each other so early in life. And then also thinking of your denial of this fine coincidence."

Giulietta turns from him and faces her mirror. She tilts her head and pulls out her earrings, sets them in a box, and snaps the lid shut.

With his elbows on the windowsill, the boy watches the ceremony she makes each night of brushing her hair. First she brushes it to her left, then she tilts her head the other way and brushes it in long strokes over her right shoulder. On his first visit, he noticed patterns on her furniture. Carved vines and blossoms smother the legs of her bed and wind over the drawers of her dresser. The embroidered rug is intricate too, and the mirror she looks into could encompass his spread arms. The mirror is clouded in places, and its edge holds drawings and notes she's tucked into the frame. Her chair is in front of a clearing in the glass that gives an exact, though amber, image. While she brushes her hair, she raises her eyes and glances at the reflection of the boy, who takes in the bedroom's details. "My sister started playing the trumpet," she whispers, with her family down the hall and oblivious of her visitor. "She's silly. She's still dreaming of…"

§

Vullie sits in the bottom rung. He claps his hands as the window shuts and the ladder shakes.

"So, did it go well? Did she fall in love today?"

The boy jumps down the last couple of rungs. From the dark yard, the window above them glows. Mazzu looks up at it and shakes his head. "No, not tonight."

They carry the ladder across town and prop it against Vullie's house. With the seaside town settling into an evening quietness around them, Mazzu takes a bag from Vullie, slings it across himself, and begins the walk home. He crosses a bridge and lingers there with his hands on the rail. Then he crosses through the marketplace while phrases Vullie and Giulietta said quiver in his mind. He comes to a cross-back stairwell matted with leaves and soil from innumerable rains. Mazzu has tried different routes home—around the path up the back of the hill and through the wooded trail and the heaps of insects—but those gentler routes were much longer. With a bag of mail for the mayor, Mazzu climbs the middle of the stairs, where the stones are least obstructed. At the top, he raises his eyes to the mayor's slouching home and crosses the lawn surrounding it.

§

Mazzu was six when his parents died. "The fire ate my parents," he told people. "But it was too full to eat Mazzu." The mayor took the boy in, gave him a room upstairs and, years later, a place in the basement where he could build a carpentry workshop. Initially, this was a hobby. The boy wandered through the mayor's house, tightening screws and oiling hinges. He took the problems he couldn't solve to the town's seasoned carpenters, who tutored him. The boy busied himself with repairs to Papa's home. Climbing up onto the counter, he added a shelf for Papa's growing collection of dishes. Mazzu would enter a room and immediately see possibilities. He took down a door inlaid with glass and carefully repainted it. He took down the mayor's bedroom door, too, and reshaped it so it closed noiselessly. Once he began making stylized picture frames for Papa and word of mouth spread, Mazzu was asked to make several more. When these were sold, he bought more tools: a coping saw, someone's mismatched chisels, and a jig. He had a workbench in the basement, a cabinet with nails and screws, a box of clamps, shelves of tools, and, by his feet, a rack of paint jars. He took measurements and, with Vullie's help lifting the lumber, built a bookcase for Papa's unruly office.

The fire had raged throughout the ground floor and basement of his home, corrupting the stairwell and the second storey. People gathered and yelled to the boy, who was asleep upstairs. Each time he appeared in the window, the crowd cheered and urged the six-year-old to jump. "It's too high. The boy will die. He should try the stairs."

"No, I've been inside. He must jump."

The boy appeared at the window and threw clothes—pants and some shirts—out of the window. The fire meanwhile lunged through rooms, crossing floors, chewing through cabinets and a table and bursting over a chair. The boy appeared again and threw more clothes from the window. "He thinks this is a joke. Jump! Forget the clothes!"

"Where has he gone now? Not more clothes."

"What if the wind starts?"

"These other houses, wake them up, get them out. Where's the boy?" The fire stalked fabric, oils, catching the floor in the hallway and tearing up the stairwell and slamming against walls. A shelf slipped from its bracket, plates and bowls falling through the hot air. He appeared again, this time with pillows tied around his body. He stepped through the window and hung from the second-storey ledge, his legs flailing, until his weak arms gave and he fell screaming to the lawn, his left shoulder crashing into the ground, snapping his collarbone. The boy stood, ripped the pillows off him, collected his scattered clothes in his right arm and walked away as the gathered crowd, stunned, looked on in silence.

§

In the basement of the mayor's home, beside Mazzu's workbench, is an abandoned jail cell. The thick bars of the old cell gate are in the shape of rasping snakes, some of their heads high up at the ceiling and others down at the ground. The barred window on the far wall of the cell lights the stone basement. In the afternoon, the light travels across the floor to the stairwell. As the sun descends, the column of light recedes back across the boy, until only the cell is lit with the evening's ambient glow. Mazzu works next to the cell, which has always been empty.

For two days, though, a man has occupied it. Mazzu has seen him lean against the wall and prop himself up with an elbow on the windowsill. He has watched the man rise from the noisy bed and walk lengths of the ten-foot cell in pants and a shirt of faded indigo, then sit again and shift restlessly. For two days Mazzu has watched him in the periphery of his vision. Mazzu sits on his stool, dwarfed by his workbench. A single lamp heats the basement. The boy works in the yellow circle of light. Each finished plaque flushes him with a satisfaction that is out of proportion to the menial task. He leans over the panel of wood and, puffing his cheeks, blows shavings away. Mazzu stands and shakes the wooden panel clean, using tasks like these as an excuse to get a glimpse of the prisoner. There is something holy in the silence between them. While Mazzu once hummed or muttered admonitions to himself as he worked, now there is silence. If Mazzu stands, the legs of his stool scraping across the basement's stone floor, the man in the cell can relieve his stinging lungs and cough. There is this timing to their relationship, this coupling of their noises so they don't intrude on the presence of the other.

Mazzu has heard the man stand and heard the clicking in one of the man's knees when he paces.

When the mayor comes downstairs to talk with Mazzu, the boy is unusually quiet, muted by the presence of the third party.

"What are you doing still working? It's late now." Papa leans over the workbench, wheezing from the descent. She looks past the boy at the man, who leans on the window ledge. Taking in his posture and presence, she gauges the prisoner.

The boy looks up but doesn't reply.

"Leave it for tomorrow."

"I want to finish this. I don't like stopping in the middle."

"Just ten more minutes then."

At night, after Mazzu has left the basement, the prisoner wanders the cell. He crosses his arms on the windowsill, listening for any sign of life. Someone passing through the seldom-used garden, an animal rustling in the shrubs, any noise to take him somewhere, to move him beyond the grip of the town's hilltop cell. The mind can go crazy in such isolation. His mind skips, revisiting past events of his life, shuffling them together, then pulls one apart from the others, using the past as a refuge against the present. The night around him is still, not a branch moving, no sound of commerce or the wind against dry leaves, just the dampness that seems to walk into his cell each evening, then into his bones, chilling him.

But now he hears someone singing outside and moves to the window and begins humming along, aware of the shape of the tune, but not the intricacy of the lyrics. *I know this*, he thinks. *Where is this from?* His mind spinning, searching for the first thread of verse or chorus. Later, still humming in the darkness, he wanders the cell, his mind dispersing like smoke beyond the grip of his isolation.

2

Vullie's bike shakes from side to side under him. He has become aware of all of Baraffo's contours. He knows which streets to take to avoid delay or traffic, which backyards he can cut through, and the best bridges to use to cross the river. There was a time when Vullie turned into a backyard and found a freshly built fence flying toward him. He leapt off his bike and rolled across the lawn. Vullie stood and stormed to the front door. "What are you doing! There was no fence before! I could have been hurt. You have to give notice to the postal company if you build a fence! How am I to know? How am I to know who has built fences? Why do you need a fence? The trees were nicer and sturdier too! And they were like a fence, only taller!" He walked away in disgust, yelling over his shoulder, "You must inform the postal company!"

Often in his daylong bicycling, Vullie is among the first to notice the town's tensions. He takes what he sees to the coffee stands and barters the information for tea and evening snacks. With the other customers, they unpuzzle what Vullie has seen that day. His last duty of his day is to hand a bag of mail intended for the mayor's house to Mazzu, who carries it up the switchback stairwell and leaves it slumped inside the grand double doorway.

Vullie climbs into the lower reaches of the mountains and follows a path through a wooded trail. The trees and uneven rows of red-roofed houses pass by his shoulder. Improvised branch-and-fabric tents mushroom up on the western edge of the town. Month by month, the encampment has grown, and now it includes roped livestock and a well. From his pack, he hands out a few copies of the day's newspapers. He also has a list of jobs people need done. He leaves it pinned under a stone. He continues on, cycling back into the town. Ahead of him, the town's river, having gathered several mountain currents, rushes through Baraffo, drawing bathers and those doing washing. After several springtime floods, the community dug an ill-fated canal.

A crumbling town. The red-roofed houses rising and falling over eight hills. A dry town. In some homes, the walls have become so brittle that only a modest weight, a rolled marble or rhetorical question, could cause a section to dislodge and fall in a sheet. In other areas, plants uncurl their arms and push through floors, so the first to wake must walk the hallways with gardening shears to clip back the renegade branches. The river scarfs the town that rests at the hip of the mountains, in the shade of broad, panting leaves.

§

Bare-armed and serious, Giulietta stands in the heat of the midday market. Around her, shoppers wear large hats to shield themselves from the sun. She pushes through until she's at a table where jewellery's spread over a towel. She touches different stones, then lifts some necklaces. She steadies the glass and catches her reflection in a hand mirror. People lean together, crowding the mirrors, bumping her. When she remembers this moment later, in the solitude of her bedroom, it's impossible for her to know how long he had been over her shoulder, just beyond the arc of glass. "No," the boy says, "those are not right for you." Giulietta tilts the smeared oval mirror, catching him in it. The boy points. "It would be foolish to not try those ones."

"Those?"

"It would be the most foolish thing you've done all day." Angling himself, Mazzu pushes through the crowd. He returns to her and hands her the pair of gold, star-shaped earrings.

"These are ridiculous," she says, turning to face the boy with the earring nearly brushing her shoulder.

"Do you want to come have a coffee with me?"

"I can't," she says, showing the boy her wrist where a red string is cinched. "I promised I would come straight home."

He looks at the string without understanding. "Just a coffee?"

"I can't."

The boy walks with her from the marketplace, past a fountain, to the bottom of her hill, where she stops him from walking further with her and waves a goodbye.

§

In the basement of the mayor's home, the man sits on the mattress, wishing it were dark and he could sleep. Or he wishes that the boy were here, just that minimal companionship, someone to share the time with. He touches the walls, the bars, and reaching an arm through the window, he stretches his hands in the air. He picks up stones from the floor. He sees the meal tray that his breakfast arrived on and tosses stones through the bars at the bowl. He sits with his back to the window. With his will and physical force having no effect on his circumstance, he leans his eyes against his hands. He gets up and paces the cell.

§

When the boy hears the mayor setting the table in the kitchen, he comes downstairs and joins her. He quizzes Papa over the dishes that were handed to her during her afternoon walk. Before Mazzu moved into the mayor's home, Papa had accepted dinner invitations and spent each night in a different home. Since the boy arrived, however, Papa has changed her routine and brought a couple of plates home each night. In the large home, leaning over the table, they eat in hungry silence. Afterward, the mayor questions Mazzu. Papa knows the boy's friends, but heard of Mazzu's interest in Giulietta only yesterday. Without go-betweens, the mayor finds the boy evasive and difficult to track. On nights when Mazzu has no other plans and feels like talking, he remains at the table. Often, he uses seemingly incidental questions to ask about things that weigh on him. Sometimes the boy alludes to decisions the mayor will have to make, other times he asks about Zuraffi's verse or a phrase he heard that he didn't fully understand. Only occasionally are the questions personal.

"How come you never married?"

"I was too young."

"You were old enough to be mayor."

"The person I wanted was from a family that would have created difficulty."

"You could have overcome that."

"Some things are still difficult for you to understand."

Mazzu clears the dishes and lingers by Papa, who washes them one by one. The boy wipes the table, collecting the crumbs into his hand.

"And you won't tell me who it is?"

"I was asked not to."

"But you see them on your walks?"

"Sometimes."

"So imagine," he says, "your famous walks, where you stop in everywhere, are just a disguise for your love and you go whistling right into the house of your beloved and sit at a table and drink tea that's made for you without one eyebrow in town going up."

"That's what *you* would do."

"No. I would marry who I want and dare people to find fault with my love."

The boy's mind absorbs everything and alters it, so later, when he is out with Vullie, Mazzu finds an occasion to say, "There are some things even I can't fully explain, Vullie. But often we must pass up those things that are best for us."

§

With the sun setting behind the mountains, Vullie walks with Mazzu down the bobbing dock and then across town. At Vullie's home, they pick up the ladder and carry it through the town's central square. They lean the ladder against Giulietta's home and aim the top of it at her window. Vullie stands in the grass, bracing it as Mazzu climbs the rungs, taps on her window, and tries to pull it open.

She hasn't changed for bed and wears the marine-coloured dress with the capped shoulders and pleats she had on hours ago in the market, when he appeared over her left shoulder and their eyes met in the smudged mirror. This time, from the corner of her bedroom, she spots him and watches him struggle with the window. He makes a face while pulling on it. "Ahh, Giulietta," Mazzu finally says, with the wind blowing in around him. "You know, even if you had the balance of a drunkard and a head the size of the moon, still I would carry a mango across town each night to see you."

Her fists come down to her sides. "Even if you were as far as a star and the sky was locked with clouds, still I would close my eyes to avoid you." She grabs the fruit from him and, pushing him, she shuts her bedroom window. The boy waits on the top of the ladder. She pulls her drapes over the window.

Without a word between them, the two boys walk with the ladder through the crowd of the town square. "Only melancholy songs for me tonight, Vullie," Mazzu finally says, as they lean the ladder against the side of Vullie's house.

§

Mazzu walks back toward the coast and the mayor's home that overlooks the foamy sea. The boy crosses the lawn, passing between the pedestals of statues whose fawning stories he doesn't care to know, and he skips up the few front steps. Stopping in the breeze, he wishes others were awake. The boy walks over to the cliff. While the mayor sleeps, and with his few friends obliged to be home, these are empty hours he always has trouble filling. Without any reason he can pinpoint, his spirit plummets at night. For him, these are hours to simply endure.

Mazzu pulls open the front door, then moves from room to room, hunting for his book. He circles the house, sweeping his hands across the table and kitchen counter, then searches armchairs and coffee tables in the sitting room. He climbs the stairs to his bedroom and lights his lamp. His room flares to colour around him. He pats the bedcovers. He does not even feel like reading. He wants conversation and activity while he is filled with the energy that powers him deep into the night.

Mazzu brings a match to a candle and descends through the house to the basement, the meagre light moving in rhythm with his footsteps. Thinking the prisoner may be asleep, he steps carefully, limiting his noise. Even the sound of his breathing, or the sound when he scratches his arm, seems excessive to him.

At the bottom of the stairs, the boy sees the man lying on the mattress. Mazzu turns back and sets the candle on a stair. His hands search the workbench and a shelf, bumping into jars and clamps.

"I hear you but can't see you."

"I can turn the lamp on."

"No. It will just make it hotter."

Mazzu hears the man turn over on his mattress. The padding shifts under his weight and the joints of the wooden supports creak.

"My book. I left it somewhere."

"It's on the floor. By your stool."

Mazzu finds it and stands with it against his side. He tries to distinguish the prisoner from the darkness of the cell. "Sorry for waking you."

"It's fine. I wasn't sleeping." The bed creaks again as he gets up. It's as if the shabby structure exhales as the man pushes his weight from it. "You're not sleepy?"

"No. I never get sleepy until late."

"Do you have cards? We could play."

Between each sentence, Mazzu is aware of the silence. In the basement, between the phrases the man utters, the boy senses the vastness outside, the field of grass on one side of him and the sea on the other.

"I played with my parents," says the man. "Whenever I was dealt a good hand, I would start tapping my heel. My mother would reach across and put her hand on my leg, silencing my knee. Do you know how to play rummy?"

"No."

"I could teach you. My father could count cards. Some thought this was cheating. Do you play any card games?"

The boy shakes his head.

"It's quick to learn. You're the one who lives with the mayor?"

"Yes."

"How come we never met before?"

"Because I live up here, I only have a few friends."

"Did you ask the mayor why she picked you? Some friends of mine used to wonder about that. When we heard what she

34

did, we wondered, why did the mayor select you? There are many people who suffer. Many children who are alone and need a roof. But she picked just one out from all of those, instead of doing something proper for all those like you."

"What's your name?" the boy asks.

"I'm Babello."

"How long will you be in here?"

"No one's said."

"What did you do? I've been living here eight years, and no one's ever been in this cell. Everyone else goes to the town jail. They once told me this gate is so old it couldn't even lock."

"Try it. It does lock. What do you do over there?" he asks.

"Repairs. I also make frames, cabinets, chairs, and wind chimes. I made a trunk for Papa too. And now she has me engraving Zuraffi's verse. She doesn't want the poems floating around and getting lost. There have been fakes. She doesn't want people misled. She wants the real ones preserved for everyone to read. I carve them into plaques and attach them to posts, and someone else puts them up around town."

A breeze whirls in and circles in the stairwell, bothering the candle. The man and boy stand in the flicker of light.

"Do you notice that sometimes Zuraffi tries a poem twice?" Babello asks. "Sometimes you can read two poems that are close to the same. She's twisted the first or given it an undertow."

"Yes. Of course."

"So, which is the correct one? When you make these plaques, do you carve both?"

"No."

35

"You only carve one?"

"Yes."

"Who judges which one is better?"

"I do. Papa gave me the job, and I do it."

"But if you carved both you could stand them on the posts side by side. Or even attach them to the same post."

"I don't want that. I want to carve the right one."

"Is that what you'd like to do when you're older? Carpentry?"

"No. I want to be the mayor. What? You don't think I can do it?"

"That's a different apprenticeship than what you've been given."

The boy looks at his workbench. The finished plaques are piled on the floor. Beside that, and piled higher, are pieces of wood the boy will stand above and carve. Each night, he sweeps the stone floor and uses a rag to clean his workbench. After just a couple of days, the man knows the boy's routine.

"Papa was only eight years older than I am now when she became mayor. Every day she's teaching me. She just brings me with her and I see what she does in different situations."

"There are many in this town who could use this apprenticeship. So why you? She must think you're special."

"Why do you say that like it's bad?"

"Do you believe the special are more deserving than others who aren't special?"

"What did you do?" the boy says again.

"She hasn't said?"

"Papa asked me not to ask, and I respect her."

"You obey her?"

"Yes."

"Like a dog?"

"No, like a son."

"But your bloodline isn't with her. It's with someone like me. We could be cousins. That's more likely than you being her son."

"What did you do?"

Babello paces, stretching his arms above his head. "Suppose there was a landowner. He bought up more and more land until the town whole was his. Then he asked us all to move to the mountains."

"That's absurd. It couldn't happen."

"Why? People make profits. People buy up land and force others to leave. Can't he tell us to live in the mountains?"

"Why would he want to live alone?"

"So, landowners keep us for their pleasure?"

"What did you do?" Mazzu asks again.

"I wanted land back."

"There are many homes, many places to live," Mazzu says. "No one asked you to move."

Babello nods as he paces. "Okay. Suppose four farmers sit down together for dinner. But only one of their farms has produced food. The other three have nothing. They watch him eat. What happens after six or seven days of this?"

"He would have to give up some of his dinner or go away and eat alone."

"But he likes talking with them while he eats."

"But he would have to eat alone if he didn't give them some. Otherwise they would just take it from him."

"Let's say one day, after months of this, the lucky farmer divides his meal into three pieces and gives it to them and keeps nothing for himself. What would happen then?"

As Mazzu imagines the scenario, it seems clear. "The other three would be angry."

"Wouldn't they overturn the table?"

"They would likely hurt him too."

"So, is that just? The man who gave up his meal was charitable. Isn't charity noble?"

"I would be upset if he came back and gave me some of his meal after months of eating nicely and giving me nothing."

"But hurting him is unjust?"

"Yes," the boy says. "He's still doing a good thing."

"And you would overturn the table if you were them?"

"Of course."

"So what good is justice?" Babello says. "Justice isn't connected to right and wrong. It protects people who have luck from others who lack it. It preserves their loftiness and soothes their conscience and protects them from having to share."

The boy raises his hands. "No, no, you confused me. I'm not unjust. I am just."

"Maybe that's because you've been lucky. Your own field grows well."

"You don't know anything about me."

"You live with comfort. There's a dinner for you every night. You don't fear having your things taken from you. You don't fear being beaten. You'll never be told to leave this town.

You want to govern and join this tradition instead of destroying it. Only the lucky could want this for themselves."

Mazzu opens his mouth to answer, but says nothing.

"But I also know," says Babello, "that your instinct for right and wrong contradicts what you've been taught about justice. And you're young. You can change."

"No, I was confused. You tricked me." Mazzu approaches the bars that divide the basement. "What did you do to be in jail? Are you ashamed of it? Is that why you're hiding and dodging?"

"I had a disagreement with someone the laws protect. Our laws are made and changed by the rich. You see that, right? They're not natural. They don't serve all people. Conscience knows right and wrong. Justice doesn't."

"What did you do?"

"Suppose I burned down someone's business."

"Why? What does that do?"

"You have to do something beautiful with this life."

"Like ruining someone else's life?"

"There are laws better than those of Baraffo. A fire can be more beautiful than any flag or song or charity."

Mazzu turns his back on Babello. He hurries up the stairs, the flame casting a skin of yellow against the walls, the ceiling, his chin, and his shirt as he rises through the house.

"Mazzu," Babello calls. "You too will make your own beauty. We all have to."

The boy is near the top of the stairwell, and about to turn into the main hallway, when he hears Babello again: "It isn't enough to endure! We all must make our own beauty."

Babello's voice follows the boy up the through the house, echoing against the walls and spreading into the corners of the seaside home. Mazzu turns the doorknob and walks with the candle into his neatly arranged bedroom.

3

Some mornings a bucket of water is left outside Babello's cell with a sponge floating in it. Babello reaches between the bars and squeezes water out over his head. He rubs his eyelids, his forehead, and wipes his cheeks. Babello scrubs himself with the hard soap, then rinses, bending awkwardly to tilt the bucket over his chest. The sheet crashes onto him, the bathwater collecting in pools to seep between the stones. Another bucket is left for him to relieve himself in. Each week a set of clothes, leached of their dye, is left with a stiff towel. The prison guard who makes this trip across town waits upstairs in the mayor's sunny kitchen.

In the basement of the mayor's house, the boy sits at his workbench, determined to ignore the prisoner. On the other side of the bars, Babello lies on the mattress. They pass the morning overlooking one another's noises—the rustling of pages, Babello shifting on the mattress, or the sounds the boy makes as he digs into the plaque, carving Zuraffi's conscience into the grain. Puffing his cheeks, Mazzu blows away shavings and wipes the half-finished plaque. He leans over his work.

With a ruler and set square, he pencils guidelines in for himself. Positioning the stencil, he outlines the letters with measured distances between them. He reaches for his knife and cuts the edge of each letter. Using a mallet, he taps the chisel along the grain or uses both hands to wiggle the chisel through the wood. When he pauses, he flexes his hands and shakes out his wrists.

Later that day, the boy's mind ripens with an idea. He envisions it, thinks through the sequence of steps, and the one problem with it that he decides to overlook. Mazzu clears space on his bench then goes upstairs. He comes back carrying a few planks. He makes more trips, stacking the wood. When he has all he needs, the boy begins measurements, then sets up the wood and saws it with long strokes. He taps the tip of each nail with his hammer. On the other side of the bars, Babello puts his book down. The boy works quickly, kneeling and moving around the floor, blunting the tip of each nail before driving it into one of the aged planks. He stops, and with his hands clasped on his head, he roves around his project. He pulls on the corners, testing those joints. In a final flurry of movements, the boy finishes and kicks the sturdy thing with satisfaction.

Mazzu pushes the trough across the floor, banging it against the cell gate, dully ringing the bars. He goes upstairs with a bucket swinging from his hands. When he passes the mayor and her inquiring eyes, Mazzu nods to the basement and tells her Babello is talking too much. "I'm putting a curtain between us. He's trying to convince me of the beauty of starting fires." The boy fills the bucket with shovelfuls of soil. In the basement, Mazzu tilts the soil out and spreads it evenly and goes back for more. Mazzu sweeps up the spilled soil and turns the lamp off.

Babello breathes in the smell of the earth rising through the air. He catches the boy's eye. "Where are you going now?"

"Courting."

"Is this done?"

"Yes."

"You're courting for love?"

"Of course for love. Why else would someone court?" Mazzu looks at the mango he turns over in his hands. He climbs up from the basement, leaving the man in the deteriorating basement light.

§

With the ladder angled against the house and braced by Vullie, there is exasperation within the creamy walls of the second-floor bedroom. Giulietta throws herself back on her bed. Her bedspread puffs up. "Why do you visit me with these words? The back of a camel? The temperament of a bullfrog? What does that mean? Why do you compare me to awful things? You should be praising me. You should be complimenting me, saying how singular I am, and maybe I should inspire you into some doubt or nervousness or inadequacy?" She gets up and slouches at her desk. In front of her is a broad mirror and a shelf with her journals on it. To her other side are stacks of paintings covered by a cloth. "What sort of courtship is this? You should be complaining about death, or saying how life is too short to express how much you feel, or how you can't even find the words that would—"

"But I've found words. I've given you some wonderful words," he says from the windowsill.

"And you should put down other girls to me too and—and compare me to beautiful things! Like...lilies or the stars or secret mountain ponds or the delicate early sun—and maybe admit the mystery I am to you? And you should come at the exact same time each day—or earlier each day because you just can't bear to wait. And you should let yourself really feel the full impact of what love means. You could stumble or tell me I'm graceful," she says, looking at her cheeks and her chin. "Or how my eyes are forever. You could call them seas or portals. Or like the sky..."

"I think it's a wonderful sentiment to say, 'Still I would visit you even if you had teeth of a cow.'"

"No, Mazzu, it's awful."

"How? How is that bad, Giulietta?"

She walks toward him, shaking her head. "It's just awful." She pushes his arms through the window. Giulietta shuts the window and draws her curtains over the pane.

She lifts the cloth and lays the paintings around her. She looks at them one by one. Those lush depictions where beauty and terror married at an apex of intensity... From a drawer, she pulls her finest possession, the only book she deigns to own. She loves it so fully she has given up all other writers as if they were mere dalliances. For her, there can only be Gaspo Ferhetta. Even the paintings she has are inspired by Gaspo's ardour. Why, she has often lamented, did he only write two books? Could it be true that a mind such as his was only capable of two true works? She unties the straps and sits with that

44

weight on her lap. Everyone else was just toiling in life's shadow. Gaspo revealed all other writing to be exercises in pretense, will, or studiousness. He alone understood the material of the heart. Even though she has many sections memorized, the twists and passion breathe bright and urgent in her. She thinks of the boy with mixed feelings. Mazzu is right to embrace the ordeal of crossing town with his friend's ladder, and he is right to pour praise over her shoulders, and she can overlook his height and shyness (why has he never once stepped through the windowsill into her room and craved the touch of her skin?). But why is he not swept away? Why is he not compelled to give in? And why does he leave so promptly? True feeling would compel him to linger and beg for more minutes…

§

Mazzu is attentive to all the sounds of the mayor's house. Each footstep bears a personality. He can hear feet cross from the hallway outside his bedroom, cross down to the kitchen and to the stone walkway outside, and know who is walking and even their mood—cheerfulness, anxiety about a pending decision, contemplative moments or joyful energy—such as when Bhara, the mayor's chief aide, walks with crunching steps onto the kitchen floor, and instead of drawing a chair away from the table or pouring himself water, stands in front of the window with the momentous tides of his own broad thought. The boy hears everything through the house—specific drawers opening and shutting, hinges, coughing, cabinets banging, muttering, even the mayor's obstructed breathing—he hears everything, save for the noises in the recessed basement.

There is the momentary jangle of a key slipping into a lock downstairs. Mazzu has tired of reading and is lying in bed, blinking at the ceiling. He waits for the predictable noises that follow. The door swings open, then closes, the lock snapping shut. He hears the familiar breathing. Mazzu changes and climbs into bed, waiting for the mayor to pass in the upstairs hallway. A rustle in the trees outside: some birds jump from the branch and suddenly squawk at each other, unaware of the delicacy of the hour. Mazzu hears footsteps on the stairwell. His hand dives out from the covers to turn down his lamp.

Papa taps on his door. A double tap, then she waits for an answer. Papa hears nothing, so she taps again as a warning of entry, then opens the door. "Mazzu? I saw your light on." The mayor enters and turns Mazzu's desk chair around. At this hour, she is slower and suggestible. She looks at the sketches he has pinned to the wall. In the corner of the room is a guitar she brought for him, but which he hasn't learned to play. "What happened to the rug?"

"It's rolled under the bed."

"You don't like it? Isn't it nice to step out onto something soft?"

"I like it like this."

"I've been thinking: you should take time off. Enjoy yourself before school begins."

"I like how it is," Mazzu says. "I just work when I want."

"But maybe you want to have fun before the fall?"

They sit in the dark with a strip of light from the hallway falling across the floor between them.

"Does the prisoner bother you?"

Mazzu shakes his head.

"Even though he talks about his fire?"

"He surprised me on the first day he was down there. I was afraid."

"Why?"

"It's his face. It's how he looks. It's his aura."

"Did he do something?"

"He's so arrogant," Mazzu says lightly. "But I was scared for no reason. How come he isn't in the general prison?"

"But he isn't bothering you?"

"No, he's quiet. He mostly reads and paces. And he just looks out of the window. I think that's why I was afraid. It doesn't bother him that he's alone and in jail."

"What do you think of him?"

The boy sits up and pulls the blanket up too. "He seems intelligent. Sometimes he gives me word puzzles."

"Word puzzles?"

"Riddles," the boy says. "That I try to solve."

"What do the riddles mean?"

"Nothing. Just word games."

"About what?"

The boy shrugs. "Little quibbles. Choices. Like, is life a circle or a line? Games like that. He makes them philosophical. How come it's better that he's here instead of the prison?"

"Bhara's worried about him mixing with the other prisoners. Maybe I'll move him to the general prison if you won't take a vacation."

"Why is he worried about him mixing? Babello's fine here. Don't worry about him," Mazzu says. "He hardly says anything. How long will he be in jail?"

"We don't know. We only just caught him. Bhara wants to talk with him."

"Did you know Babello before this?" Mazzu asks.

"We met once. He went missing the day his class was reciting the Sixteen Laws. When he turned up again, some teachers pulled him outside and waited for him to recite them, but he sat on the grass until it was dark. When I walked by and saw what was happening, I asked them to let him be."

"But everyone has to recite the Sixteen Laws."

"No, everyone has to live by them. He hadn't done anything wrong."

"But everyone says them."

"That isn't compulsory. It's a rite. It's an honour."

"It's supposed to bind us to others."

"It's enacting those laws in your life that binds you to others, not saying the words. He does regard other people's suffering as his own. He does try to alleviate suffering. He doesn't bear hatred. He does try, in his way, to make the town better. He does wish for good."

"He bears hatred," the boy whispers. "And that's the first law that the others follow from. He's said he feels hatred. And that's against the fundamental law."

"You have to think about more than just words. If what he hates is suffering, that isn't hatred."

With a silence hanging between them, the boy asks Papa when the last time was she saw Babello before he was imprisoned.

"Last year he was handing out pamphlets. When I questioned him about it and heard his replies, I asked him to run against me in an election. He refused. 'And what happens to us if we lose? You don't care about us,' he told me. 'You want to win and vanquish our message and make us seem small so you can finish us off.' I couldn't convince him that this wasn't true. I tried to tell him it was important for the whole town to hear what was upsetting him."

§

After the mayor goes to bed, the boy is restless. He stands in front of his window with his hands clasped on his head. Stepping into the hall, he listens outside the mayor's bedroom. When he was younger, Mazzu spent sleepless hours walking in the dark, opening drawers, and peeling back rugs. He thought this was the sort of home that was filled with trap doors and concealed treasures. Mazzu peered behind paintings and felt with his arm behind bookcases that leaned from their walls. He looked through the kitchen cabinets and flipped through puffed-up books. He used to go through the house searching for openings to a wilder life.

Mazzu takes a deck of cards from a dining room drawer and walks downstairs. The glow of yellow sharpens against the opposite wall of the stairwell as he descends.

Babello props himself on an elbow as Mazzu settles on the floor. Mazzu takes the cards from the pack and hands them over. Babello shuffles and deals an open hand while he explains the rules. Mazzu impatiently waves off a second open hand. Babello shuffles the cards against his pants leg.

"You're wide awake?"

"Yes."

"We can play to five hundred, then."

The boy reaches for the upturned card. Later, when Babello discards a queen, the boy rebukes him. Mazzu lays down his hand, capturing the first round. "You should pay attention," the boy says, gathering the deck.

The hands of cards are dealt at a steady pace.

"How did the courting go?"

"Just pay attention to your cards," Mazzu mumbles. Later, still thinking of Giulietta, Mazzu thinks of a trade he can offer. "Are you married?"

"No."

"Do you know anything about love?"

"I am engaged."

Mazzu takes a breath. "Could you tell me about love? I don't know anything about it. If you tell me something real about love, I'll tell you something that's helpful to you."

"Why? What have you heard?"

"You'll be moved to the general prison soon."

"When? Why aren't I there now?"

"Bhara says you'll poison them. It's overcrowded. Those old horse stalls aren't meant for so many. 'Store the flint away from the explosives,' Bhara said. He wants to keep it peaceful there. Bhara's very heroic. That's how he talks. That's him being normal and talking normally."

§

As they're finishing their game, Babello puts a finger to his lips, motioning the boy to silence. Babello points to the lamp and gestures, so Mazzu leans over to reduce the flame.

There are voices outside, a young couple walking through the terraces of the town's wedding garden. "No, it was lovely," they overhear a woman say. "I love that song toward the end."

"How does it go?" a man's voice replies.

"It's something-something, 'Roses for you in winter.'"

"The sugary one!"

"I like it," she says. "But I forget how it goes."

"It's roses. Something with roses in the spring."

"Yes," she says. They are leaned together against the wall of the mayor's house.

He sings softly.

> *All through spring,*
> *Among heaping rain,*
> *I'll come with roses*
> *And make my gains.*

"Yes. And the rest?"

> *And all through summer,*
> *Damp in the heat,*
> *I'll come with roses*
> *To quicken your heartbeat.*

> *And in the fall—And in the fall—*

His singing falters. "I forget that one," he says.

"Almost. You nearly have it."

"'And in the fall'—I know it. I can hear it.... 'In the fall'..."

She coaxes him, humming...

"It's been so long," they hear his voice say.

Babello jumps to his feet and is across the cell in a couple steps.

> *And in the fall,*
> *My welcomed calls,*
> *And the complaints we'll bear,*
> *From loving everywhere,*
> *Yes, you'll be one of the few*
> *I bring my red roses to.*

They turn, and in the moonlight, they see his face behind the bars. Though he smiles, his eyes and voice frighten them. They hurry from the garden. Babello raises his voice. Checking over their shoulders, they see the window and the man behind it still singing, but louder now, to reach them.

> *All my calls—*
> *So you know it's true,*
> *It's only you,*
> *I bring red roses to.*

Babello is still, leaning his head against the bars. He turns back to the boy and crosses the cell. "The Saccharine Love Song," he says.

4

From the dusty streets of the town, some of the people of Baraffo look up at it: Zuraffi's tower in the sky. The red-brick column rises above the surrounding homes. Plump birds nest on those ledges. For those who walk below, the tower's blue-painted interior gives a certain illusion, an illusion of sky. Zuraffi's existence passes for months at a time without incident and she abstains from the usual sign of renown in the town: a sententious, tutoring bearing. Townspeople speculate on the nature of Zuraffi's character. Some assume she lives with such stringency that even her day's breaths are counted and allotted; others suspect her of egoism and accuse her of irredeemable sins; most simply think of her as a rare bird sustained by a wholly separate diet.

Zuraffi's home was once a clock tower—a monument rising above the trees and the roofs of the town. Then, during one invasion or other, the giant hands were torn down and used as weapons—several townspeople steadied the minute hand on their shoulders before crashing together through barricades. Once that incursion was repelled and their victory cheered, the clock face was torn down and displayed in front of the mayor's home as a reminder of their town's eternal struggle.

It was in that courtyard in front of the mayor's home, with the hedges, statues, and propped-up clock face, that Baraffo's unorthodox elections occurred. The aggrieved, as well as those who simply came to relish the spectacle, gathered around the incumbent mayor. Sitting on the ground and the available benches, and perched in the overhead trees, the citizens of Baraffo berated the mayor with questions, worries, and the growing threats to their peacefulness.

It was as a spectator herself, decades ago, that Papa stepped forward from the crowd as a usurper against a moustached incumbent. She rose from the grass and walked forward, dressed in her only suit, a white one garnished with a daisy. Many cheered the audacity of her challenge, while others, appalled at her presumption, tried to hold the young woman back. The sitting mayor looked at Papa first with bemusement and some paternal affability, and then, an hour into their debate, with scornful affront. After duelling for ninety-five minutes, the sitting mayor sensed the unmistakable tide of adoration that was buoying this talented upstart, exchanged a look of defeat with his wife, then formally announced his withdrawal, declaring the young woman Baraffo's freshly elected mayor.

As an incumbent herself in the years that followed, Papa continued this election procedure far longer into the evening than previous mayors, talking into the cool night air to extinguish all doubts and assess all accusations. These elections were held at irregular intervals, either when the pool of the aggrieved had grown to a worrying size, or when people became nostalgic for a display of the mayor's virtuosity, or when some townspeople contested the stories of the mayor's successes. "Rumours!" these bony-faced critics cried, "Fantasies! A concerted propaganda!" until the people of the town, having no other recourse and aware that this could not continue, rang for an election.

Two days before each election, Papa would move into a friend's spare room. Unable to eat, she drank sweetened coffee in the purity of solitude. When she washed, rinsed her black-stained mouth, and emerged from this two-day isolation, the townspeople would greet her with a rare formality.

The gathered people hushed and the squawking birds were threatened into silence. When the twenty-six-year-old mayor stood before them for her first bid at re-election, the townspeople sat through this initial phase of the afternoon in silence until one citizen leapt up and, possessed by some spark, challenged the resolute incumbent. The canal was filthy, she said, and without enough flow. After her, a shy man unfolded a page and read a delicately worded second question in a trembling voice. Wild cats, he stammered, were a menace to those who lived on the town's edges.

Over the years, a pattern was established. In that first hour, Papa would begin carefully, speaking with deliberation, plying the ears of the crowd with the music of a soft-spoken diplomacy. Some people likened her opening technique to that of a seasoned chess player who advances their regiment with discipline. After an hour, the mayor had her jacket off, her sleeves rolled up, and she was in a contented sweat, pointing new challengers out, allowing glimpses of her famed show-manship. Late in the second hour, amidst the clamour of reactions, with her broad smile unleashed, she picked her way through the ailments and inequities voiced by the crowd. And in the third hour, convinced again of her destiny, Papa worked boldly in the courtyard, dismissing some challengers with a smile, a wink, the majesty of her historic hand on their shoulder, others with pointed single-sentence rejoinders, and the remaining few she froze and made pale-faced by announcing the conflicted truth of their existence with the rough honesty of plain language.

Those spectators who lounged in the trees with napkins of food in their laps murmured election commentary to each other, and, straining to hear all the comments in the courtyard beneath them, they marvelled at the scope and suppleness of the mayor's knowledge. Papa was in full style by the end of the day's election, leaving the doubters vanquished, pointing out new challengers and working her way through the towns-people until, in early evening, with the enchantment of the sinking sun, ardour erupted through the civility of the cere-mony. In the roar of the courtyard, the hugs and heaped flowers, and amidst apologies from the disbelievers and the zealotry of the enthusiasts, her triumph was broadcast throughout the town, and, as the first minutes of her renewed term began, the people of Baraffo cheered, laughed, applauded, and marvelled at how one of their own could have gained such wisdom, humility, compassion, and panache.

After six of these victories, and with Papa visibly aging, the citizens believed that these elections were an unnecessary duress. They were generally understood to be in bad taste. So, the people of Baraffo stopped calling for them. The mayor didn't take this as an act of mercy. She assumed it was a sign of town-wide contentment.

§

Alone in the mayor's untidy bedroom, Mazzu pulls open the bottom desk drawer and sifts through a mountain of keys. He walks with his glass of water down the hallway, slips a key into a lock, and pushes open the door of the library. Light falls in from the window at the far end of the room, and over a gold-upholstered chair. Aside from the collections of anonymous folk tales, the library holds drawings, letters, the account of a large shell arriving on the road one day, philosophical tracts, diaries, portraits, erroneous maps, nautical charts, architectural drawings, a drawer of recipes, cascading family trees, and a shelf of songs and poems with their prying commentaries nestled alongside them. Mazzu has read about how the river used to bloat, bulging over the banks and islanding the town from the greater land mass. He has pored over deeds, reliable drawings of various seeds and trees, and failed amendments to the town's fundamental laws. On a low shelf he had to crouch to examine, he found a sheaf of papers covered in a tumbling script in a pattern that looked to him like knotted hair. He couldn't tell if it was art or language. He once dragged the padded chair across the library floor and, stretching up, unlatched a box of assorted stones and vials. With his thumb, he nudged the corks from the glass mouths and tentatively sniffed them. Beside that, a heavy-lidded box contained the wills of prominent townsfolk. The boy sat with that folder on his lap and read through these precise, nearly inhuman documents, and learned that this house he was in had been donated by a family as a residence for the town's succession of mayors. He wondered how long he and Papa would live in that house. Where would they go if someone else were elected? Even though he disliked that they were beside the sea and far from the possibilities of the town's centre, the boy couldn't imagine living in any other home.

The boy has thumbed through everything in the packed shelves of the mayor's sealed library, heaving dust into the air. The family trees of his friends and people he has met—trees a generation or two out of date, so they hang in time without their living branches. He has wiped dust from portraits and studied their dated expressions. Because the past is exotic, he has even read a pile of papers that explain arcane farming techniques.

If he hears someone coming up the stairs, the boy closes the door and waits for the footsteps to pass with the trove of documents glowing against the walls around him. One day, Papa noticed the boy in there, leaned in, and asked Mazzu to be careful. "Some of these books don't have second copies yet."

There are two items the boy wants this morning. He finds a copy of the folded political pamphlet Papa mentioned the night before and leaves it on the puffy seat of the chair. He rummages through his pocket, finds a nail, and uses that to mark the spot on the shelf it was in. He steps forward, his finger cutting across the dust of a shelf, brushing along the wall of books. He stops at a ruined spine. As he pulls the untitled Gaspo Ferhetta volume, folded letters fall from the cover.

He gathers the private documents, pausing to read several paragraphs, then the dedication page of the volume—*for the truest of true souls, the undaunted lovers, the breathers of truth, and the embracers of full dignity.* As he skims the pages, he becomes sure of his hunch. He flips ahead, and his eyes pass over the extravagant gestures, the secrecy, bad luck, and the patter of infatuation. Though the realization makes him ache, the boy is sure: contrary to what Giulietta and Gaspo both believe, real love, love that is wildly alive, overflows all boundaries and manners and includes all aspects of life—humour, joy, gravity, but even debasement and vulgarity—love includes all states, not just the fitted clothes of solemnity.

He holds the book open and has the letters in his lap. His eyes pass over the fanciful names of Gaspo's kindred characters.

What is a mazzu anyway? he wonders. He thinks back to myths of the ancients who fell from the sky, marrying and mingling their customs and histories. And those travellers who bombarded the coastal plains where the town would later rise, mixing tongues and features. From which line did his name originate? What did it express? The boy looks around the library, hunting for a possible definition among the shelves, then thinks of his work area downstairs as a source of possible clues. The many jars of paint that crowd the shelf below his workbench—perhaps it's a colour? Mazzu, some subtle shade. Or that strange tool he found a couple of days ago and brought home. That could very easily be a mazzu. Setting down the book, he picks up his glass of water, finishes it, and turns it in his hands. The remaining drop of water slides around the bottom of the glass.

§

In the kitchen, Bhara, the mayor's broad-chested chief aide, finishes his customary midafternoon snack. The boy often passes him during this daily break and is always surprised that such a large man could satiate himself on a sandwich no bigger than the ones Mazzu makes for himself.

Bhara eats his sandwich at the kitchen table, facing the window. He is proud that even the sight of nature—even if he is indoors!—replenishes him. ("So many people lack this sensitivity," Bhara once lamented to his wife.) The light from the kitchen window, and this break in the middle of his usually contentious workday, refreshes him. Weeks ago, through a combination of self-assurance and rigour, Bhara broke through the top echelon of the mayor's advisors and captured the position of chief aide. After this promotion, he spent all of his afternoons in Papa's home, attending meetings, influencing her schedule, and privately counselling the mayor.

Before Bhara's arrival, it had only been the mayor and the boy in this spacious house. Some days, the sole contact between Mazzu and Papa had been when there was a knock at the door, and the boy would run up, pull the front door open, and guide the guest to the mayor's office. Mazzu would linger at the door, eavesdropping as some conflict was explained to Papa. But with Bhara spending his afternoons in the house, and with the prisoner locked in the basement cell, the boy adjusts to the crowded home and the trample of footsteps and voices. Besides the prisoner and chief aide, there are other newcomers. The arrival of Babello in the basement cell brought a couple of uniformed guards who check daily on their prisoner. They look into the cell and test the gate. And in the afternoons, Bhara brings his own retinue: students, professors, and other followers trail after him and offer their counsel.

§

Over the sea east of Baraffo, fronts have collided. One slips below the other and rushes to shore, the wind spreading through streets and trees, driving against homes, against tents, against hung laundry, rocking the moored boats, rushing up steps and rattling the town's thousand windows. Wind pushing against a bedroom door, squeezing between the door and frame, releases into a narrow room and pushes against the corner of a page. Mazzu shifts position, pinning the corner down with his thumb, and sinks further into the persuasions of some of the letters. A breath of wind around the edge of the door spreads through the room and is released through the open window, wandering Baraffo's streets.

That day's unusual heat changes the boy's routine. Restless and unable to concentrate, Mazzu traverses the house's main hallway on his way out to search for Vullie, but realizing that this early in the day he would not even know where his bicycling friend would be, he pauses. He deliberates on the rug that runs through the centre of the house, plants unfurling on either side of him, and weighs his choices. He thinks of Babello, who has begun abstaining from the trays of food that are left for him on the boy's side of the bars. The last couple of days, the trays remained overnight. Mazzu lifted them away in the morning.

Mazzu shakes his head as he trudges down to the basement. He flops onto his stool and faces the cell. "It is good that there is this basement."

"This air," Babello says from his side of the bars, drawing a breath deep into his lungs, "is so heavy today. It must be a thunderstorm later."

Mazzu wipes his forehead.

"How is it out there?" Babello asks. "What's happening?"

"Oh, everything is out of order, Bello. Birds are diving into the river to drown themselves. The fish are jumping out and cooking themselves on the rocks. Anything to escape this heat. It's all out of order, Bello."

With the basement dim and humid, the boy leans back against the bench and watches Babello walk the confines of the cell.

Babello notices a low mood in the boy and tries cheering him up. "I've been thinking that I will grow a beard," he says, rubbing his cheek.

"People may mistake you for an intellectual. But you could walk around in public as though you were guarding secret wisdom. 'Fierce intellectual,' they will say. 'Babello, the fierce intellectual.'"

"I wouldn't mind that."

"But you could never smile. A smile would surely show your lack of wisdom."

"You could join me. We could be the fierce intellectuals."

"Maybe in some years, Bello. It would be improper for me to fake wisdom so young. When I am your age, perhaps I will.

I would grow a long one so that if I were walking down a stairwell I would be in constant danger of tripping."

"But if you did trip you would curse and become bitter. You would be so miserable from all the tripping that people would think you had more intelligence than they themselves had."

"But what if someone told a joke, Bello? I laugh easily."

"Who would risk telling you a joke? You'd make it clear you didn't have time for any humour or casual talk." Babello sits on the mattress.

"Feel like playing cards?" the boy asks. "I haven't been able to do anything today. It's just too hot."

Babello comes over and sits at the edge of the cell with his legs stretched.

"Is there anything you want?"

"Yes. Some water."

"You're not hungry?"

"No."

Mazzu hands him the cards and walks upstairs. He pours water from a pitcher and carries the glass to the basement, where he passes it between the bars. Babello drinks quickly, wiping his mouth and chin against his shoulder, then pours some water onto his shirt and uses this to cool his face. He sets the glass down on Mazzu's side of the bars. "You must have been thirsty," the boy says, picking up his cards. "Look. Only the mazzu is left."

"The mazzu?"

The boy nods. Mazzu shows Babello the glass. "That drop of water that stays in the glass. Come on, let's play."

"I've never heard that word."

"It isn't common. For some, that's part of the delight."

"Is it only used with water?"

"Most commonly, yes. The poets, though, they can use it many ways. Many ways, Bello."

"The mazzu. It doesn't sound poetic."

"Oh, it is poetic, I assure you."

"So, it's a quantity of measure?"

"Yes, exactly! A quantity of measure! Come on, let's play."

Babello looks around the basement. "The evening's mazzu of sunlight?"

"Yes! The mazzu of sunlight! That has been used in many poems. Many poems, Bello. It is almost cliché. The poets love to welcome dusk with it. They can't help themselves."

"The mazzu breeze, moving against me?"

"Many poems, Bello! It's an extravagant thing to say."

Babello picks up his cards and looks at the pleased boy.

§

"What do you have now?"

"Two hundred and ten."

"I have 340."

Babello checks the upturned card and selects from the deck. "I once liked her poems too," he says. "They made me feel still and placid and they made me search myself. But too often she sings about inner life rather than the life people go through here. Even her love poems are philosophical. They are not about a real person. Zuraffi shies from life and what goes on. She just adds to the delusion. That isn't something to admire. Especially from someone who's important."

The boy's knees are almost bouncing on the floor with excitement. He shakes his head. "But politics is only important to some. It's true! Go to the coffee stands. When you hear people's grumbles, there is philosophy underneath it."

"Every poem is political. Every story. What is loved? What is praised? The luxury someone has? An attitude or posture? A sense of leisure or recklessness? All of these things have a source. They don't come from nowhere. They come from the conditions of someone's life."

The boy's rebuttals have no effect on Babello. He simply shakes his head at what the boy says. "You're young, Mazzu. But you'll see. Philosophy is just an innocent form of politics."

"So, what about love then? Do you believe in love, or is everything logic and arithmetic to you?"

"No, I believe in it."

"You do?"

"Of course. I'm engaged."

"You were engaged," the boy says. "Now look at you. What good is the promise you made to her now?"

"I'm marrying her when I leave here."

"So, what is it you love in her? It's impossible to believe what you just said and also to believe in love. What did you say to her?" The boy laughs. "'All of the things that come into being in me love all of the things that come into being in you?' This is love? You would say this to someone?"

"I could say something like that to Isabella with my full conviction."

"She wouldn't be happy with you. Even I know that."

"Of course she would."

They continue playing cards, gathering their hands then emptying them onto the floor. "No, I think you are too sensible for real love," the boy says. "You're backward: in politics you dream, and in love you reason."

"I don't dream in either of those realms. I notice and I act."

Mazzu has learned that Babello becomes careless in his play when he speaks. When the boy is within striking distance of winning the game, he searches for a topic to distract Babello. "Bello," the boy says, scratching his head, "I feel I can say this to you now. We're becoming friends, aren't we? So, I can say this. What you have is a fool's grin. It's ungainly. You'll never have a trusted position in this town. It's as though your jaw is unclasped from your face. You have no other face then—it's all grin. The one you just had was subtle and, let's say, civil. It has some dignity, and you don't look ugly. But the other one, when that happens, there's nothing pleasing in your appearance. It's foolish, and your face loses all sense of proportion."

"Say what you will, but this grin has got me further than your mangos ever will."

"Isabella is nice?"

"Yes."

The boy looks at his cards. "So, you traded in looking at her nice face every day to look at mine instead? Bello, if someone nice ever liked me I would *never* trade her in to look at your face." Mazzu picks up the card the man has discarded and, laughing, lays down a run of spades. "Tomorrow maybe you will win. It's mostly a game of luck, no?" He slips the deck back into the pack, and then flips the cards onto his workbench, before picking up the empty glass and walking toward the stairs.

"Mazzu?"

The boy turns. Babello is still sitting on the floor with his legs stretched and his face neutral. "Is anyone speaking out there? In the town? About my fire? Are people talking?"

Mazzu shakes his head.

"There's nothing? Really? How could that be?"

"But how do I know, Bello? I spend all day up here."

"Could you ask friends?"

The boy shrugs.

"You won't, will you?"

"I've been asked not to. "

§

The sea waves berate the rock wall and hurl themselves against the shore. On the streets, people hurry home, looking at the sky. The boys sit in the wind on Vullie's roof, outside his bedroom window.

"Should we go to Giulietta's?"

Mazzu shakes his head. He holds his hair back with both hands.

"I don't mind. We could be back before the storm starts."

"No. Not today."

Vullie lies back on the roof with his hands under his head.

"You know, she never once said thank you. If someone brought me a gift, I would thank them. I wouldn't throw it from a window. I wouldn't do this in front of them."

"She's not the same as us. Look at her house," Vullie says.

"But I live in the biggest house in the whole town."

"You do carpentry there. What does she do?"

"I just do it for fun. Just yesterday Papa came asking me to stop, but I don't want to." Mazzu sees the moon, which is orange on the horizon, below the masses of clouds. "You don't think Giulietta has any hobbies?"

"She's different from us." Vullie glances over, but even that recognition does nothing to lift the boy from his dejection. "You don't want to go to her tonight? There's nothing you want to give her?"

"There is one thing. But it will have to wait. I can't give it to her when it's going to rain."

§

In the basement of the mayor's home, Babello leaves the mattress and stretches out on the floor. The coldness from the stone rises into his back and arms. The moonlight comes in through the barred window and stripes him. He waits. The night wind is a reprieve. Babello overheard a fragment of dialogue what seemed like hours ago and constructed a story from it. Anything to lift him from seclusion.

Outside, the wind builds, pulling on clothing, bending trees, collecting debris and fallen leaves and driving them against the other side of the stone wall that Babello presses his palm into. The wind pushes up against the river's current, knocking boats together.

The first thunder. He props himself on an elbow. Lightning sweeps a moment of daylight into the cell. Shadows spring to life, race across the wall, then die.

The rain drums down and swells into a storm, polishing stone, stripping branches, the rain falling in sweeping sheets, covering Baraffo. Babello jumps to his feet and reaches his arms between the bars, catching water in his cupped hands. He gulps back handfuls, the water running from his chin to his stomach. He rubs his hair and face and the back of his neck, and swallows more before washing his arms, his legs, and his dusty feet. Between gasps, he yells for the boy. "It's raining, Mazzu! I was dreaming of this. I was praying for it. Can you hear me up there? I was dreaming of all of this water." He carries more water to his hair, cooling himself until he's slick and clean. The light from the moon shines against his hands. "I was just dreaming of this and wanting this more than anything—more than any meal or wine! More than comfort or pleasures I was dreaming of a long rain! Can you hear me?" Tilting his hands up, he slurps back more. "Are you awake up there?"

Four friends rush home, crowding together under a couple of umbrellas. As they cross the public garden, one turns her head and sees the silhouette of two arms, impossibly long, reaching across the horizon's bloated moon. She watches the thinness of those limbs scissoring against the light. For a moment she thinks those arms divine.

5

Morning spreads across Baraffo, drying leaves, fields, and the stone walls of the mayor's hilltop home. The first pots of coffee are made. Some houses are awake. Families sleepwalking down hallways and into kitchens bump absently into each other.

Mazzu climbs onto a chair and unfastens the drapes in the living room, which spent the night absorbing rain. He spreads them over the grass. He walks around them, pulling their corners, then squints at the sky.

Downstairs, Babello scratches the wall with his thumbnail then blows the dust away. He has spent seven days isolated in the town's seldom-used cell. When he is on his bed, his mind ventures. He recalls the events and atmospheres of various nights. He remembers debates with his friends and the energy of the argued ideas, the crowded planning sessions, the large meals made in cramped kitchens, the feeling that surged during their gatherings, and the early mornings with Isabella.

When Babello's request for a pair of scissors is rejected, the boy brings him a pair that is almost useless in Babello's beard.

His hair bends over the blades instead of cutting. With his thumbnail, Babello tightens the bolt binding the blades, then works the scissors over his chin. Babello lifts a corner of his mattress and wedges the scissors there, where the guard can't spot it.

The boy comes downstairs. He points at the tray of food.

"You won't eat this?"

"No."

Because the coarse material of the prison uniform hangs stiffly from Babello's shoulders, it's difficult for Mazzu to notice the impact of his fast. "Should I leave it here or just take it?"

"You can take it."

Mazzu carries the tray upstairs. He leaves the peach and torn piece of bread in the kitchen for others to pass by and pick over.

§

It is late in the afternoon when Babello tries once again to speak with Mazzu. On previous days, it felt like the capacity for laughter was tumbling everywhere within the boy. But today he is remote, his expression closed, and he offers little emotion.

The boy sits at his bench, unsure what to do with a knot in the wood of an uncarved plaque. He looks down at the pile and sees a knot in the next one too. The boy flips through his pages for a poem that could work in those impaired plaques. He shakes the debris of his carpentry off of his clothes and arms, and cleans his bench before resuming work.

"How come you're so quiet today?"

"I'm just tired," the boy says. He wipes his face. He shows the plaque to Babello, who reads it and passes it back.

"I know that tiredness. Who are you tired of?"

When Babello asks if the boy wants to play cards, Mazzu agrees. He returns the tools to their places on the shelves and hands Babello the deck. He sits at the edge of the cell and, for the duration of their game, he tries pushing back against his mood. He steals a glance at Babello's hand and sighs. "When are you dropping that seven?"

"You're looking at my cards?"

"The way you hold them I can hardly avoid it. You should really drop the seven. You have no need for it."

"Now I'm keeping it forever."

"This is just silly. You need a three of clubs or a ten. The seven, though, is of no help to you."

"You realize that you're not supposed to be looking at my hand?"

"So now the criminal is lecturing people on rules?" The boy laughs. When he regains himself, he sees Babello staring at him. This is the face that frightened Mazzu the first few days Babello was in the cell. It took days for the anger to drain from his pointed jaw. Mazzu looks away, picks at his cards, and then glances back over at the man, waiting for his face to become more human.

"Sorry. We can play a new hand."

"No, let's continue."

"I'm sorry."

"It's fine."

"How come it angers you to be called a criminal?"

"It isn't what I am."

"How? How aren't you a criminal?" Mazzu whispers. "You even confessed. You did a crime and you confessed."

§

Giulietta waits in her bedroom without changing. She spritzes the air with a perfume. She looks at her window when she hears a rustle outside. She finally gives up waiting for him and gazes out her window. *What did I do? Do I deserve to be ignored like this?* She thinks of his freedom, and all the possibility it must bear. What has he found that's more worthy than her? And why is he so obstinate? Why won't he understand? Isn't that love's prerogative? To understand and harmonize with love's course? Or is he unworthy of that pitch of devotion? Is he just fickle? Is he even capable of melancholy—that palpable proof of depth? With her mind ricocheting through different explanations, Giulietta finally changes for bed. She lifts off her dress and lays it over the back of a chair. With her head on a purple pillow, she wonders where in their town he is at this moment. What would happen, she wonders, if she crept down the hallway and out of the front door? Is the town's nighttime crime as alarming as her parents have warned? They have bred in her a fear of thieves, kidnappers with their ransoms, and grosser violators. She pulls the covers up and lies there and envisions how he will quake when he next sees her. She will single him out, even if there are many others around. Then she imagines washing away from everyone on a gorgeous river of wine and giving herself over to the current's "blissful decisions." That drunken episode in Gaspo gave her an artful ache....What it must be, she thought, to die for love. Would Mazzu even care if she died? She knows one thing: he lacks the nobility to cap his own life and brocade himself in such exalted symmetry. But would he have the decency to properly mourn her? Or would he just move on? Giulietta remembers when she would cross the hall on troubled nights and nestle alongside her heavyset grandmother.

When she hears a second sound from her window, she props herself up, then walks over to the window. She pulls it open and leans her head out into the darkness. What she finds is a nail driven into her windowsill. A packet hangs from the nail. She takes it, unknots the twine, and spreads the letters on her bedspread. She reads through the pages with confusion. They are old love letters infused with an urgency that beseeches, begs, and pleads—all for a single thing: for the beloved to throw off their dearly clutched pretense, be sincere, and step forward from the shadows. Something in the language of the beloved, who insists on the necessity of the guise, nags at her. She knows the breathing style of that prose. She knows the blood of its consciousness and its gait, even if this is her first time reading these private compositions. After completing a first reading, she shuts her eyes as hot distress overcomes her. She opens her eyes, and her bedroom and life are much the same, but, for her, all is changed. She reads them through again as the wild emotions of her realization vie in her. Gaspo Ferhetta, her dear guide, her lamp through what she understands about humans, and the pinnacle of a life of courage, was no recklessly obsessed man, but a calculating woman in hiding. Her beloved addressed her only as *Dearest P* and urged her to abandon the silly moniker....Her name was not even real. It was all an illusion. There was nothing authentic about her. Giulietta reads the letters through a third time to weigh if forgery or imitation is impossible, and her fourth reading is spent consolidating the facets of her spreading revulsion. She takes the leather-bound volume from her drawer and checks the prose against the letters. She flips pages and pulls a different letter near. Though the panache is muted, and the high-toned imagination suppressed, there is no mistaking the voice. The document she found most authentic, the embodiment of what she most adores, is pure, untested fantasy. She pushes the book and letters to the floor.

Giulietta lies in bed. On her back in the dark, she turns on herself. What does she really know? What knowledge does she have that is firm and true? She searches herself and her life, but she can't think of a single thing.

§

In the basement, Mazzu turns the lamp up. The grey stone walls take on a gold hue. In a sunken mood, Mazzu has avoided Vullie and Giulietta and the mayor today. He sits on the floor, quietly playing cards. "What is she like?" Mazzu asks for a second time, wanting a distraction. "Come on, I told you they're moving you to the prison. Now you have to answer me."

The lamplight glows against the bars, and on Babello's arms and neck and the side of his face, which has darkened with the beard.

"You promised."

Babello straightens his legs. "I was always finding new sides to her. I woke one day and the room was bright, the sun coming through her curtains, heating everything. I turned over and there was a row of jars along the window ledge. They were jam jars that she rinsed and filled, a clipping of a different flower floating in each one, leaning this way and that. She put tape on each jar with the name of the plant on it. A row of cut stems, leaning against the lip of jars she had rinsed and saved. I pressed my thumb along the edges of the tape that curled free of the glass."

"Plants can grow in water alone? I've never heard of that. Maybe it's like plants that grow on the ocean."

"No, those are attached to the floor."

"I'll find some jars and try that. My own love life," Mazzu admits, "is sputtering." He pesters Babello and pries into the prisoner's past. His awareness that he is missing entire swathes of knowledge fills him with shame. "How did you meet Isabella? You've known her for long?"

"No, it was just last summer. I wonder how you remember that time. The summer of drought must have been very different up here." Babello waits for Mazzu to reply, but the boy waits. "It's so hot now," Babello says. So the boy turns the lamp down. The light in that space collapses. There is still the hum of the lamp consuming its oil and, above that, the noise of breathing.

"The worry everywhere was the farms and their starved crops," Babello says. "The drought came and the fields of vegetables wilted and shrank back into the ground. This is what you've read. How the price of vegetables tripled. But the

76

heat was making people crazy. Everyone was fighting and cursing. I was in school then. One afternoon I was studying when the one summer rain came. I jumped up and looked out the window. The rain fell and evaporated instantly, the latent heat of the ground boiling Baraffo dry. And us, walking on the cracked ground, bracing for the food shortage, wanting to tear away our layer of skin as though it were a sweater. Walking across the steaming ground from study groups, peeling off clothes to jump into the thinning river, wade out into the current then allow it to swing you through Baraffo.

"At night, we could no longer buy anything at the morning's price. Even as you bargained with the merchant, the price rose. Whatever food you held in your hand mounted in value as it became rare.

"The nights were best. Everyone awake past 2:00 a.m., finishing chores they could not do during the day's heat. Studying, meetings, the vending stalls, opened and lit by a row of communal lanterns. All of us awake past 2:00 a.m., past 3:00 a.m., waking at eight when the heat was already unbearable. All of us delirious from the heat, delirious from the lack of sleep, finishing all of our studies by midnight so we could launch into the parties that filled that summer. The conversation swinging wildly as we all looked for logic to the summer's disorder.

"There was one man who found logic in Zuraffi. He cited her work, claiming she had awakened a demon that was tormenting Baraffo. He showed how Baraffo's demise came as the poet gained her strength. He climbed onto a rock or crate on one block or other pleading with the passersby, reading sections of her verse, waving his arms, crying, then reading from some other text. Linking art with dormant mythology. The people gathered, some beginning to believe in him, finding plausibility in his arguments. In spite of his efforts, though, he wasn't able to gather enough support, and he was jailed shortly after plunging a blade into the poet's thigh. The heat was making everyone mad. But now the reason isn't hard to see. It was just a drought.

"Those nights were best. Talking until we were drunk, until the bottles were dry, then talking until we were sober again. I met Isabella at one of those parties. I had known her before; we spoke briefly after a play she was in, but never much. Then that night, it seemed she was always there. Whispering some sarcasm into my ear, taking me to meet her friends. And she turned and I would be close by. There was suddenly this nearness. As though she were always within arm's reach. I don't know what changed. I could reach behind me and pull her into a ring of conversation and she would bounce in rhythm with us. She might have spoken with many people that night, but this is how I remember it. This was when we were all drinking heavily and would meet the next day and put together all that happened on the previous night. We would wake with bruises or scratches and need someone else to explain what had happened. I've since become wary of those who drink heavily.

"Yes. That's how I remember it. A sudden nearness."

§

Upstairs, Papa sits at her desk in her cinched robe, organizing her thoughts while she composes a letter. The light falls over her shoulder onto her hand, her wrist, and the filling page. The room around her is quiet save for the scratch of pen against paper. Her dull ears don't catch the boy's footsteps climbing the stairs or coming down the hallway. The ink slips across the page, flowing at the pace of her thought. Something wavers and falls in her mind. Papa spins around, snatching her glasses off, and sees the boy standing only feet away from her with his hand out, trying to calm the startled mayor.

Mazzu waits for Papa's reaction to taper off. Papa takes a sip of tea, runs a hand through her hair, smoothing it into place and sits down again. Turning the chair to face the boy, she apologizes.

"Are you busy?"

"No. You frightened me. Why are you still awake?"

"I was calling you from the door, but you didn't hear me. I even knocked."

Papa clears papers and folders from an armchair. She pats the cushion. "Here, sit."

Papa watches Mazzu walk around the office. The boy picks up an old medal, reads the inscription on the back and slides his thumb over the engraved surface before replacing it. He walks the length of the mantel, gazing at the objects crowded along it—mementos, gifts, drawings, and piled books. On the shelves, stacks of paper loom behind Papa.

"Come. Sit, Mazzu. What is it? Why are you still awake? What's wrong? How have you been? Why did you miss dinner? You saw that I left it for you, right?"

Mazzu turns away from the objects he has been examining and sinks into the armchair. He looks at the windows at the far end of the office and sees, in its dark panes, the reflection of Papa and himself and the lamp.

"What is it? What's bothering you?"

Mazzu pulls his elbows in from the armrests, which are too far apart for him to sit comfortably. He turns to Papa and leans back. "Tell me about Babello."

PART 2

6

Katrina had been a joyous mother. She celebrated Anavo's milestones with splendour. Each of his birthdays was a little carnival, with musicians, a play, stilt walkers, and, on two occasions, caged mountain animals. Believing that the worst quality in a boy was meekness, she knelt to each of Anavo's needs and nurtured him into robustness. Her son would never address a room with a quavering voice; he would never vacillate over a difficult but necessary decision. She admonished any sign of shyness. While he slept, she came into his room and whispered praise into his ears. Catching the reflection of her and her son in a mirror one day, Katrina felt a tingling pride. He was her dream, her ideal. He was clear, bold, and self-possessed. In the evenings, after leaving work, she sat on his bed with a book in her lap and read him parables exalting courage and ferocity. With his sharp face, the boy lay in bed listening to these stories, receiving the lessons with attention, so that by the age of ten, he was ruthless, efficient, and he had a reservoir of conviction. Anavo bathed on time and without fuss, observed adults with an unsettling stare, spoke flatly, his speech torn clean of the enthusiasm of adolescence, and he espoused a liberal, though pragmatic, mindset. Through these years, though, Anavo's unspoken desire was to fly.

In secrecy, Anavo trapped insects in a handkerchief. Once he heard the fluttering cease, he lifted the cloth and peered at the beetles, wasps, and butterflies. Through his friends, he put a bounty out for captured birds, and when they were brought to him, he unwrapped the newspaper and felt the architecture of their wings. He possessed the logic of mathematics without the clumsiness of numbers. He discerned ratios between wing breadth and weight. He pinched wings and understood patterns of cartilage that gave resilience against storms. Anavo went to the town's carpenters, inquired about the varieties of wood, their weight, tensile strength, and cost, then built several gliders. He climbed to his second-storey roof and flung them off. Other boys followed the flight of his gliders and shoved each other to collect them from the lawn or tree where they landed. He sat at the riverbank and made notes about the flow, threw leaves in to see how water behaved around bends, and how the fluid reacted against rocks and counter-currents. He used these observations to predict the behaviour of winds.

After months of this private study, in the unsupervised hours before Katrina arrived home from work, Anavo changed into old clothes, pushed his bed against a wall, and began work on a pair of elaborate wings. He shaved the wooden frames thin and stretched fabric over them.

Though often tempted, he never confessed his ambition, those around him dismissing his solitude as that of an unusually private intellect. What Anavo wanted was to fly across Baraffo when crowds filled the roads and parks to watch the sunset. He would be a graceful silhouette and land somewhere in the length of the river, skimming into the blue.

When Anavo stood on the roof and reviewed his plan, he became frustrated by the wind's irregularity. Even on days when the gusts were ample, tugging at his pants and sleeves, he found that just minutes later they would slacken, making his imagined flight fatal. He paced the roof, evaluating different solutions. It bothered him that he would be dependent on such fickleness. During dinner one evening, Katrina mentioned someone who had begun a third marriage. Anavo shook his head. "People are as erratic as the wind. It is ridiculous we must depend on them." She smiled across the oval table. Even this precocious misanthropy she loved!

What he wanted was to shock Baraffo by gliding over it before slipping into the river. The throng of people would rush at him, fully clothed men and women abandoning conversations to dive into the water and pull him free. He imagined himself struggling to remove the giant wings while he bobbed, all those around him demanding answers, and him shrugging, wiping water from his face, and confessing, "I simply wanted to fly." As a late amendment, he desired a liquor to drink at the height of his leisure, mid-flight, once the success of his achievement was ensured. This would not only add a certain sophistication but would also relieve the pain the block of river would inflict during his entry. In the days before his flight, he sold several gliders and used the money to buy a vial of ruby-coloured liquor.

On the fateful day, sitting in school, Anavo provoked other boys. He raged. He threw a book. His teacher came over to him, rubbed his shoulder, and spoke with such kindness that Anavo behaved himself. After lunch, when he was in the midst of a second willed tantrum and he overturned his desk and tore his collar, the boy was ordered to go home. Anavo ran through the streets. Once he was in his bedroom, he pulled his wings out from under his bed, examined their joints a final time, and rechecked the details of his plan.

Anavo climbed to the roof, hauling the wings one by one up the stairs, and immediately noticed the flourishing wind. He thanked the sky. He flung several gliders off the roof and watched them coast far longer than he'd hoped. "Yes," he murmured, watching them waver on the unseen planes of air. Using stones to hold the wings down, he lay back on them, knotting the ropes at his waist and under his arms. He tugged the ropes, testing their knots. He had imagined he would have time for deliberation, a moment to savour the anticipation or look out at the town, but when he felt the gusts pushing him, he clutched the vial and struggled against the wind to the back of the roof. Anavo ran the length of the house and leapt.

He captured the wind, his neck pulling back; people below startled and pointed at the strange kite. He resisted acknowledging them, locking himself on the angle of his flight, his mind ripped clear of friends, memories, the essential wisdom encased within the holy parables his mother fed him. There was only an appreciation for the fists of wind that drove into the fabric, lifting him above the town's commerce.

Anavo rose into afternoon flight.

He climbed into the sky above Baraffo and, tilting his arms, rose above Zuraffi's red-bricked tower. The separate plots of lawn passed below him. He could see the mountains, the streams that glinted, the distant farmlands to the north, and the sea, brilliant and dotted with cliff-edged islands.

Anavo fought for breath. Lowering his chin to his chest, then his shoulder, he struggled to inhale the hurtling air, which came at him too fast to be faced directly. With the town fleeting beneath him, his spread arms split the sky. He shuttled forward on the wind's volition with the vial in his fist. He could barely inhale, and then there was his new concern that the tarp could split, flinging him into a spin.

The wind swivelled and pushed another way, knocking like a heavy hip against him. His eyes streamed with tears, but his mind was preoccupied, fixated on the river and the possibility of unknotting the ropes before landing so he could tumble deep into the water without the obstruction of wings. So, as he veered, he was not unsettled. He corrected his flight by leaning back against the burden of the current. The wind sighed, preserving his precision, before regrouping and overhauling him. Bracing the ropes against him, the boy rolled through the air. The fabric fluttered, but held. Anavo muscled his left arm down.

With the wind bursting like a wave, Katrina's son rode the air in swerves over the mesmerized, open-mouthed town.

Once the thunder began cracking, Anavo was cursing. His arms fought to regain his line of flight, but he was unable to prevent a fateful veering or achieve any deceleration. The haven of river fled his line of vision, and the sea was behind him.

When he realized his flight was doomed, he snapped the vial between his teeth and swallowed the liquor so that as he skidded across a series of roofs and the length of a lawn, stopping only once his head split a flowerpot, he was wonderfully drunk.

Only two people were there in the yard when the town's postal carrier arrived. Vullie cursed and backed away. He pedalled across town and up the mayor's hill and returned with Mazzu, who circled the mess. The boy extricated one of the wings from a hedge while Vullie turned away from the growing crowd, which was lauding the young corpse as the first of their people to fly.

Atop Vullie's roof, Mazzu marvelled at the wing. Kneeling over it, he studied the craftsmanship.

Midway through that evening, the people of Baraffo wondered if Anavo had, in fact, been some ill-fated angel. They clustered and debated his fall. "Who did he betray?" someone asked. "And why must angels fall?"

"Where else will we one day go?" another man asked, raising his eyes to the stars.

Katrina's marriage dissolved. Those near her, thinking they were doing good, amused her with stories, philosophies of chance and mortality, distracting pleasures, sang songs of consolation, tempted her to swim, but they failed to unbutton her from her unbearable coat of sorrow. She cried for weeks, saying nothing at all while her son's life story was reshaped by the buoyantly chatty town. While deep in grief, Anavo's life morphed into a town-wide lesson promoting reasonable limits and the importance of laughing off one's own ambition. Katrina, meanwhile, wept without control.

Without any place to be downcast, Katrina fled inward. She swallowed her parables and retreated from her circle. Life, she was sure, lacked solace. She had nothing to say to anyone. She reduced her activities to her life's most basic functions and completed only those tasks that were required, so, a year later, when a ponderously large man named Bhara was introduced to her, she was a woman of no pretense or enthusiasm. She dressed in muted clothes, wore no adornments, and her manner had neither aggrandizement nor humility. She presented herself factually, accurately, and her talking was not strained by drama, emotions, or comedy. Listening to her, Bhara found her remarkable: She was perfectly impartial. Her perceptions enthralled him. Leaning forward in a chair that looked far too small for him, Bhara did not interject or tell counter-stories. He was charmed. He held her hands. He never thought he would meet someone so placid, even, and pure.

The extent of his ardour worried him. In the initial phase of their courtship, when he was apart from her, Bhara was shocked at how often he thought of Katrina, and in the afternoon, when his energy dipped, he worried that she wouldn't requite his affections. Even at that stage, only weeks after meeting, he was sure that Katrina would be an essential part of his life. There was no mistaking this.

He brought her gifts that she liked not for their own value or charm, but for the childlike energy that glowed from him as she thumbed the ribbon aside.

Katrina had no wish for a prolonged courtship; they were married within months of meeting. And Bhara did not pry into her grief and never did what irritated her most: he never inflected any of what he said to her with solemnity, sympathy, or condolence. Without those reminders nagging at her, she could dispose of her life's tragedy the way she liked: she ceded her airborne boy to the town's repertoire of gossip and lore.

Bhara was a sturdy, optimistic presence beside her. Living with him almost immediately, and absorbing the self-assurance of this man who seemed to exist without any pessimism at all, Katrina began to warm.

Bhara had to be the largest man in the whole town. One night, Katrina measured his back while he slept. She spread her hands and walked them across his gargantuan width, touching her thumb to her other thumb, then swapping her hands, and touching little finger to little finger. Six. Sitting cross-legged in the dark and in awe, Katrina measured herself. She was just two hands across.

All it took to remind her of his nature was one look at his clothes or at how he carried himself. He was always clean-shaven, he kept his fine hair precisely parted, and his attire fit him perfectly. It took weeks, though, for her to understand the depth of this severity. Bhara bristled at any offer of dessert, so she gave up dessert too. He permitted himself only two extravagances. One of them was his endearing habit of giving Katrina a one-on-one retelling of the entire sequence of his day. The other was his gardens. His front garden was grown to a height that shielded his two-bedroom home. The back garden, with its two beds of flowers, the single tree that he pruned by going up and down on the stepladder, and the vines that climbed the fencing, was an enclosed idyll where they could sit after dinner. He had purchased a home well within his means and showed little interest in decoration. Save for books, his walls were bare, and he didn't clutter his shelves with curiosities or ornaments.

"This town," Bhara once wrote to her, "never changes. It's like a still water pond, or a fenced garden—like a family that does not move apart." When she read these words, which felt as if they came from inside of her, Katrina's affection for him became involuntary. She wanted to seize him and dominate him, and also, brimming with adoration, to yield completely. She became fastidious with her clothes and hair, and she read more and tested her growth in conversations. She reflected on this new element she found in her, this fire, and felt that this feeling was what others termed "passion." She thought this to herself at thirty-seven, years after she had resigned herself to a cooler existence.

In the first year of their marriage, Bhara's abhorrence for the chatter and morning noise of the town's tax office reached such an extent that, once he had earned a sterling reputation for his work, he refused to leave his house before lunch. Katrina enjoyed these consecrated elements of his life, the absolute stances he could take, those habits or decisions that were non-negotiable.

She understood that others found him unbearable—she wasn't blind, she was sensitive enough; she could see what they regarded as his faults. He was no diplomat. In fact, his personality had a brutal aspect that could leave people cast aside like unearthed trees. He was incapable of measuring his speech to the occasion, he would never go unseen in a gathering, he would never dazzle her with spontaneity or excite her mind with a surprising streak of humour, but there was no doubting his goodness. He never trumpeted himself the way other men did. What pride he had was proportional to his standing, he was scrupulously honest, and he didn't brag about his physical strength. Physically, Bhara's chest and shoulders dominated him. It was a quality retained from years earlier, when he swam daily and wrought himself into maximum form. Some evenings Katrina lay against his bulk, desiring only the comfort of his mound of shoulder.

Bhara was an autodidact who disciplined himself from feeling contempt of others. He openly challenged his peers at the tax office. With his voice and confidence, he intimidated people without being aware of it. Despite his deficit in hours, Bhara maintained an acceptable level of productivity. He refused offers of promotion. He was keener to offload responsibility. Then, just before his fortieth birthday, after reviewing his savings a final time and with Katrina's blessing, he went into work and negotiated his retirement. His colleagues were baffled and affronted. Bhara was done writing nagging letters and creating graphs. He was done being a go-between for the money that circulated. He was done listening to jokes and personal pleas and complaints. When pressed for a reason, he attempted to mask his joy and assume a grave demeanour. "You diminish me," he said. He tutored his colleagues in the processes he had overseen, and then he walked out into Baraffo's afternoon sunlight. *This is all glorious*, he thought. The sky was blue, with only wisps of cloud. *All this. There can be nothing more wonderful than this little world.* With his newfound freedom, he walked home that day through the brightness of the market in disbelief.

Bhara's mission was to read each book in the town's library. He made a list of them and pinned it to his wall. He wanted to be the embodiment of complete knowledge. As he progressed, he took the page down from the wall and crossed each title off with a ruled line. As his knowledge accrued, essays began stirring within him, then two longer treatises: one on false education and the forfeiture of one's self, and a second, darker treatise on the seductive appeal of social joy. The town and its people surged through him and inspired his thought.

When he became lauded for the singularity of his opinion, he was welcomed into new circles and a university post was opened for him. He spoke before a room of attentive students. Only the self is permanent, he said, and only that deserves nourishment. Nothing should impinge on this, he said, patting his chest, our sole source of freedom. Freedom begins here, he said, patting his chest again, and here—he tapped his brow. The greatest purpose and most refined one is solitude. Communities debase us. They falsify our behaviour. They lure us into hidden scripts and theatrical exchange. They dilute our essence and corrupt us. We should aspire to be independent, fully alive, and free. He was a radiant teacher. Their eyes followed him, hung off his attractive silences, and swallowed his wisdom. There is no joy, he said, more rewarding than private pleasure. This can only be attained once the social pleasures have become relinquished. He crossed to the other end of the room. Before you accomplish this, you are nothing more than time's martyr. He paused to add gravity to this final statement. Several students rushed home and sought out their private pleasure.

When Bhara became concerned that his growing body of philosophy lacked proof, the former tax officer wrote a one-page letter to Papa, offering his mind to Baraffo's aging mayor for a nominal salary. The town's turmoil was obvious. Everyone could feel the bristling. It was an opening for him, the merger of his energy and thought with the mayor's influence and stateliness. The mayor wrote back and welcomed the self-taught scholar with characteristic warmth. Bhara's first successful initiative was changing the mayor's routine: he bargained Papa down from her afternoon walks through the town. He had to make the mayor's weeks more efficient. It was long overdue. Bhara informed the mayor that her walks diminished her stature, which in turn diminished her leverage, while also chipping away at her most precious resource: time. "This town is growing," Bhara said. "Complex decisions need to be made. There is information you won't receive from conversations. The town is too big now to react to and solve as you once did. You need time to read and plan and imagine. Who are we? What are we becoming? What will we be in five years? Then, what decisions will bring us there? This should be your priority." In a back-and-forth that impressed Papa, Bhara succeeded in limiting the mayor to twice-weekly strolls. The mayor smiled to herself. His reputation befitted him. He was deeply unusual and ardent.

Bhara spent his first days in Papa's governing circle listening, his judgments and preferences obvious only from changes in how he stood or expressions that altered his face. But when their trust became palpable, and with the mayor's prodding, Bhara was forthcoming and offered his directives with concision, so that when Babello was roughly apprehended and interred in the unused cell of the mayor's house, Bhara was at the apex of his influence and had already begun focusing his intellect on questions of altruistic crime; its nature, motive, and patterns of occurrence fascinated him.

What makes someone willing to dispense with their life in an act of altruism? Egotism, Bhara theorized, or even despair at one's self. The social, he thought, as a refuge from the rotted personal. Perhaps Babello craved popularity. No, mere popularity was out of proportion with the sacrifice he made. What a martyr seeks is significance. Bhara tapped his knee with a pencil and smiled. Yes, meaning. Meaning, meaning, meaning. And so they grope for salvation far outside of themselves. These thoughts had been elaborating themselves in him for weeks. Bhara drew a flow chart and wrote pages of notes and arguments and formed the skeletons of theories. Sitting in the town's library, he felt as if his chair were poised on a cliff. There seemed to be so little documentation of this topic. Altruistic crime, Bhara whispered to himself, in disbelief and shaking his head. He was fully alive with this pursuit. How can they toss their life away?

Once Bhara heard that Babello had ignored his food for a week, he summoned the superintendent of the prison. The superintendent welcomed this midday walk across town, and also welcomed the chance to formally meet the colossal man and chat with him.

Based on a rumour, the superintendent and his colleagues at the town's general jail had a particular image of Bhara. What they had heard was that during the summer of drought, during that season's epidemic of crime, hearing footsteps in his hallway one night, Bhara lunged from his bed, catching the bedsheet with him, and swung a backhand that cracked a trespasser across the cheek. Bhara dragged the lifeless man through the kitchen and out of his house. The staff at the general prison was not concerned with the minutiae of the story or whether Bhara's actions afflicted him with guilt, but rather the justice of it, and whether Bhara deserved censure. For a week, the staff argued joyfully over this conundrum. The topic filled all of their breaks and lunches. "If any man or beast comes into my home, I will do just like Bhara," one jailer said, swinging his arm in demonstration. "Do it, fine, but don't tell us and brag of it. If it's a hot-blooded act, let it be hot-blooded, but don't make a rule of it and demean this whole system!" The superintendent of the jail sat among his debating subordinates with complete delight.

§

As the superintendent leaves the jail and crosses the town to meet the mayor's chief aide, he sees a stick. He picks it up and taps it against his uniformed knee as he walks and sings to himself. Someone stripped the branch clean of its bark, so it is white and smooth. When the superintendent arrives at the mayor's house and climbs the stairs, he listens to Bhara's request, and asks for clarification. "What is it you want, exactly?"

"Speak with Babello," Bhara says. "Find out why he isn't eating. Appraise him. See what he's like. Discern his values. Be discreet, but take his measure. Give me his portrait. What drives him? Is he cunning? What is he hiding? Then come and report to me."

The superintendent looks at Bhara's hands. One holds a saucer and the other a dainty cup of tea. The superintendent nods and descends the two flights of stairs.

On the eighth day of his incarceration, Babello looks over his shoulder. The superintendent stands at the snaking bars in his olive uniform. With flair, the superintendent jams the stick into the trough's soil and faces Babello with his fists on his hips. During their exchange, the superintendent asks the boy to leave the basement for a few minutes. "No," Mazzu replies. "I'm in the middle of working." And he continues to carve a plaque while listening. Still facing the boy and his workbench, the superintendent observes the distance from the boy's bench to the iron bars, then pivots on his heels and glances at the length of Babello's arms. Satisfied that the prisoner can't grab anything of worth from the workbench, he takes his stick and climbs the stairs to the chief aide's office.

"He seemed to mock me."

Bhara glances at the soiled end of the stick with anger. "What do you mean? Did he mock you or didn't he? What did he say?"

"He kept misconstruing what I said. He was evasive. It pleased him to be clever. And the boy mocked me too."

"The boy's just like that. But what did Babello say? What was he like?"

The superintendent takes a deep, deliberate breath. "Since in a sense I am your senior, and also since I bear no motive, let me say this: move him. Lock him up with the other prisoners.

It would be good for him to rub shoulders with the people we have in the general prison. It would humble him and prevent him from feeling like he's special."

"How many disturbances did you have last month at your prison? Babello whipped up a crowd once. He encouraged people to loot and steal. What would he do in your prison? How much unrest was there this month?"

"None that we didn't quell. None that we required help with. But Bhara, why is this one different? Bring him to me. Why do you keep it so dark here?" Bhara kept the shade drawn over the window. The light stung Bhara's eyes when he read the bone-coloured pages of the civic paperwork. "Listen to me. Madmen do a crime, they come to my prison. Poor people do a crime and they come to my prison. The vengeful and jealous, the impulsive and negligent, and the cheats too—all of them—they do a crime and come to my prison. But this one does a crime, and he comes here. So, it is either the mayor's special motive or yours. And since you are new, I assume it is your influence, but it's wrong. You will see. And how long will you have my guards running back and forth across town to cater for him and bring him some special bathwater?"

"This wasn't the purpose of your visit with Babello. What—was he rational or emotional? Was he strategic?"

"Let Babello rub shoulders with some of the people I have at the prison. Let him be degraded. Let us regiment him. What are you afraid of? Visit Babello yourself. Talk with him. And if I'm wrong about this, I will resign. All of this is second nature to me. I know all the ailments and which ones can run a course and which ones are doomed. This isn't someone you should isolate. This is someone you should humble. Rub dirt in his face. Let him feel small. Let him grapple with being ordinary."

Bhara dismisses the superintendent. As he repeats these conversations to Katrina at night, these frustrations spread through him and cue a nightmare. He forgets the nightmare upon waking, and it would be lost forever beneath his steady waves of thought, were it not for a single, serendipitous clue.

Having finished his morning coffee, Bhara leaves the kitchen and closes his office door behind him. Sunlight pours through the blinds, falling across him in bars. He sits distracted, fascinated by the yellow bars that curl over his arm. He withdraws quickly. The light slides off of him and rests heavy and immaculate across the raised desk. With his mind startled, Bhara watches those strips of light.

"Are you leaving soon?"

Katrina raises her eyes from her breakfast, surprised to see him leave his office at this early hour.

He takes grapes from the bowl. "I can walk with you," he says.

"Yes. Just give me five minutes. Where are you going?"

"To the mayor's house."

"The mayor's house? Why so early today?" During the night, she felt him shuddering in his sleep and shaking their solid bed.

"I have to talk with that prisoner. I can't put it off. I just can't."

"It's best that way. It's best for all of us. The more control you take the better we will be. Papa—she's too good-natured. She only sees with one eye. She doesn't see all of human nature."

99

"I'll have a talk with him," Bhara says, holding the door as she passes.

The morning outside is cacophonous. Vendors howl and people yell their greetings. "Everything is as I remember it," Bhara says to Katrina, nodding. She holds his hand as they pass the scents and allures of the market stalls, the displays of fruit that have been piled into blocks of colour, and the young guards who straighten up when they see Bhara. "It will not always be this good," Bhara says, squinting. "It is impossible. One day I will be callused to all these joys." He angles his body so she can pass ahead of him, through an opening between vending stalls. He steps through it sideways. "These mornings are just as I remember them." With his hand at her back, he escorts her up onto a higher road. "Just as I remember," he says to a joyous Katrina.

7

With a leather pack slung over his shoulder, Mazzu climbs a dirt path from the seaside up to the mayor's home. He rounds the house and goes down the stairs. The day's young light warms the basement. The boy climbs onto his workbench. He kicks off his shoes. His fishing rod is across his knees. The boy smiles at the mirrorless haircut and uneven beard trim Babello gave himself.

"So? How are you, Bello?"

The boy's radiance and out-of-breath energy lure Babello, who turns from the window. "I was alienated this morning," he says, battling his hunger.

"And now?"

"Now I'm better."

"I managed to skirt alienation this morning. Evenings are my concern. Nighttime is what crushes me. That's when I can feel doomed. But Bello? You have some fame now. There were three people who wanted to meet you this morning. They said that you are a boat. They admired you, but I didn't think much of them."

Babello's eyes harden and his expression changes.

"They said that most people simply drift, but that you caught the era's wind. We were very serene, Bello. My friend borrowed his uncle's rowboat and we were fishing, then when we were tying it up to the dock they came and ruined all that. They must have heard that you were in this cell and that I lived with Papa. They called you a boat and talked about winds and how we will all be in the future. One kept asking me what you were like, what you have said to me, what you would like someone like her to do to help." The boy towels his neck. "How is it already so hot today?"

"What did you tell them?"

"I told them the truth. I told them how you are a fierce intellectual. She was very grave, Bello. Very grave. No humour at all. She nodded, crouched near us, and talked for a while. She was very passionate. She talked about subservience and how to live with loftiness and asked me to imagine how it could be. Then my best friend asked if he too was a boat. Vullie doesn't have the same tact as I do. He's rougher than me. But it happens that that's really a main tenet of her philosophy. We're all boats! 'Most drift around, but some find the wind.' Vullie and I weren't fit for such a sombre revelation. She liked you, though. She wanted to meet you, but I told her it wasn't a good idea. That you didn't permit visitors or well-wishers."

"What else did she say? What did she want?"

"She wanted me to pass messages to you. I told her to go through Papa or Bhara. What kind of person comes and involves me? What kind of person asks me to betray Papa? Papa's given me everything." Mazzu shrugs. "It discredits her sanity that her and her friends could find me fishing at that hour. It was only just morning, and they came creeping down the dock, calling out for us. But I suppose it discredits our sanity that we were out there so early." The boy shrugs again. "Such is life."

He jumps down from the workbench, but instead of leaving, he lingers. He rubs his hands, which are tired from the oar. From the cell, Babello notices the indecision that hampers Mazzu. He questions the boy, who replies with a sigh and a shake of his head. "Something's changed. Something's different. People are emotional. It's becoming crass to tell jokes. People don't laugh anymore. They find jokes contemptible. And you're being idealized. It isn't just those three from this morning. There's a song people remade. In the chorus, they sing your name over and over again. They've made a story about you. I smiled when I heard it last night. I smiled because I was happy to be living next to the name in the song. I liked hearing your name," he says quietly. "It wasn't you. It was your name, but it made me feel proud, even though it shouldn't." Mazzu picks up the song in a register that's too high for him and falters over the tune's hills, straining to reach faraway notes. "And people know about your hunger strike. But…how? I haven't said anything, and neither would Papa or Bhara. But somehow, people know and are talking about it and they want to know what will happen to you and if they'll let you die. Did you tell people you were going to fast when you were caught?"

"No."

"Then one of the guards?"

"It only takes one person, then it flies through this town."

After the boy has left, Babello leans in the window with his elbows on the ledge. He can hear the boy outside, splashing his feet with a bucket of water.

§

The mayor's chief aide closes the door loudly behind him and hears Papa humming in the kitchen. Bhara strides across the aching wood of the hallway and into the kitchen, where the mayor is splitting eggs above a noisy pan.

Bhara pulls a chair out for himself and sits. "I asked the superintendent of the jail to visit Babello yesterday. But he isn't discerning. He was useless! He couldn't read into Babello. And he's thin-skinned. Babello and the boy both insulted him."

The mayor looks over. She goes over to the stairwell and calls for Mazzu. The boy runs down to her.

"Did you insult the superintendent of the prison?"

"He bumped into me when he came into the basement and didn't apologize. His hand knocked my head as he passed me," the boy says, gesturing the action with his own hand. "He should have apologized. Then he asked me to leave when I was in the middle of working and not disturbing anyone. It's my space. That's my space more than his. You said that to me. He came into it, bumps me, then asks me to leave. This isn't fair."

Bhara nods, sipping his tea. "He's right."

Papa nods too. So, Mazzu goes toward the stairwell, but instead of walking down, he tucks himself against the shadowed wall.

"So, what are you curious about?" Papa asks Bhara. "He confessed to lighting the fire. He implicates no one. He did this without duress. Witnesses confirm this. The only strange element is how berserk he went when the guards touched him. Once they let go, he was fine. So, what more could you want from him?"

"Isn't it our responsibility to understand him?"

"Our responsibility is to have faith that he was the one who burned the Peach Building. Then to find him and lock him up. That's our responsibility."

"He admits guilt, fine, but isn't there something greater that justice asks of us? Doesn't it bother you to know that we couldn't summarize him? If someone asks us why he did what he did, what answer do we have? How is he fine with throwing his life away? Also, he didn't give an apology. He only confessed. He refused to apologize. Why would he refuse this?"

"We don't need an apology. The confession is what we need."

"I even dreamed of him last night! I think we should make an effort to gain full understanding. Then justice will be complete. I also want to persuade him to give up his hunger strike."

"Let him cool first. Let him soften."

"What if he dies?"

"That would take a month. But do what interests you. Don't feel limited. But I think you will be disappointed. People aren't as philosophical as you wish. It's enough for people to know a crime was committed and that the criminal is locked up and receiving due consequences."

As they do with everything nearby, the boy's ears feed on this conversation and blend it with what he already knows. The way he walks into the basement, his gait and gingerness, informs Babello to keep quiet.

Mazzu used to envy Vullie and his other friends, whose homes were clustered in the centre of the town. Each night, Mazzu trudged up the zigzagging stairs back to the mayor's home, where he lived cloistered from the surprises and activity of the town. He sensed he was missing out. But with Babello growing thinner in the basement, and the mayor and Bhara mapping a plan upstairs, the centre of the town has shifted to the hilltop and the drafty home poised above the shore.

The way Babello leans, the light from the window crests his head and back.

"You're like a king, Bello. None of us can touch you. Not the guards. Not Bhara. Not even me. I go up and down bringing you water when you need it, as if I'm a servant. And people look at me differently now. They talk differently to me. They hang off me as if I'll spill your secrets. Because they know I'm near the king."

§

After nine days together, Mazzu and Babello's side-by-side existence has developed a routine. When Mazzu comes down the stairs in the morning, Babello is sitting on the floor, his legs stretched while he reads. With Babello's porridge untouched and cooling on the wooden tray, they pass the mornings together in adjacent solitudes. The boy selects a poem, clamps a plaque to his workbench, and carves letters into the pale wood. Meanwhile, the prisoner flits between reading and dissipating his restlessness by circling the cell. By midday, conversation begins, and continues until evening, when Mazzu leaves to eat with the mayor and see Vullie. At night, after the boy has left, a plate of vegetables arrives on a second tray with a heel of bread. The last couple of days, the meals have become more enticing. An apple joined the breakfast, and a broken tablet of chocolate was left with the dinner. Babello ignored these. When the boy returns to the mayor's house again late at night, they play cards, their voices echoing up the stairwell. "You don't like fruit or chocolate either?" the boy asks, twisting the stem off the apple, splashing his glass of water on it, and taking a bite.

One day, Bhara walks into that mutual morning silence, with the boy on the stool, dwarfed by his workbench, and the prisoner on his back, balancing the book he holds open on his stomach. Bhara's breadth accentuates his imposition. Mazzu senses the giant behind him. He turns and looks up. The chief aide has a stillness and majesty to him; it looks to the boy as though it would take a significant wind to knock him over.

For Bhara, the basement's atmosphere of industry is an unpleasant surprise. He imagined pestilence and neglect. But instead, what he finds is cleanliness, brightness, and an air of productive cordiality. On the floor are piles of plaques. Surrounding Mazzu is an area of wood shavings that give off a noble smell. Bhara inhales it. The dimensions of the cell please him, though. It would make him feel wretched for his shoulders to be so constricted. If it were him locked up, his composure would fray.

Bhara looks back at the boy, who leans forward on his stool to leverage his weight. Work elevates the spirit and ennobles the mind. Why does the prisoner deserve to be near this enrichment? Bhara sees the crude trough and drops to a knee.

"This is good soil." Bhara passes his hand over the trough's wood and pulls on its joints. "This is nice. Rustic."

"I built it myself."

"How did you prevent water from leaking?"

"I didn't. I'll just be careful when I water it."

"You haven't put seeds in yet?"

"No."

"What will you plant?"

"Vines."

Bhara brushes his knee as he stands, and as an afterthought, asks about the boy's motive.

"He got polemical one night," Mazzu says, gesturing toward the prisoner. "I think vines will make a nice curtain. Then there would be his side and mine."

"He bothers you?"

"Just once. But even then," the boy whispers, "I provoked him. I was curious. He was like an animal that I poked and prodded."

"There isn't so much light here. You will have to be careful which seeds you select. I can draw up a list if you like. In my backyard, I've covered two fences with them."

Bhara glances at the prisoner and sees Babello stretched out, immersed in a book the boy brought him, the spine cracked and folded so it can be held with one hand. From where he kneels on the floor, Bhara's eyes sweep the cell. He notices wisps of grass in the cell floor, rising through the crevices and sprouting from the walls. He sees nothing to inflame his concern, save for the prisoner's demeanour, which is remote and resolute.

Babello's cheeks are hollows, his collarbones leap from the shirt, and in Babello's ankles, Bhara notices twin spots where the pulse throbs.

Mazzu turns on his stool and leans over his workbench, giving Bhara and Babello a minimal form of privacy; the illusion that his mind is elsewhere.

"I heard you weren't eating. Is it the food? I have the influence to change that. I could ask them to bring you slices of chicken or fish, or something that agrees with you. Would that suit you? Perhaps you still find this unfair. But, this is the appropriate consequence." When Babello remains quiet, Bhara continues. "This fast of yours informed my dreams. I recognize the absurdity of this—that I am here because of a dream. But I've noticed in my life that my dreams have a prescience to them. So, I assume that dreams are another means of apprehension to which the intellect is not yet privy." Standing in front of the iron bars, divulging his night's dream to someone who is not interested, Bhara feels absurd. "I began my usual morning and didn't remember the dream until I was at my desk and the sunlight was across me in bars. I have blinds in my office. The sun fell through them and onto my arms and my desk. That was when I remembered you."

As he speaks, Bhara taps each of the bars with his knuckle. The iron rings dully. Then he jerks the metal gate. It wrenches forward and shakes in its frame. Dust falls from the ceiling. Babello sits up—the boy makes a face, then blows the dust off his work and brushes a hand through his hair.

"But my dreams are caricatures. Composites. They don't square with reality. What I dreamed is that you starved yourself so thin that you slipped between these bars. And I chased you through the town. I watched you walk between hinges and cracks of doors, but when I followed you, you would turn sideways and disappear. Understand, of course, that I realize the absurdity of this. Only in a dream can you vanish. But what I want to say to you is that it is enough to dedicate your life to a cause. You don't need to die for it. We believe different things. We have different notions of what makes a life worthy. But something binds us too: we dislike aspects of this town and want it to be different. Live, and enact your beliefs. If you make this fast a contest of wills, you will die. You will die without children, without a family, without saying goodbye to people. You may take pride at what you've done, you may feel you've made an impact, or made a statement, or that you've become significant, or that you've given your life some meaning, but be cautious about pride. Everything is forgotten. You will be forgotten. Don't live to be a memory. Death from starvation will take three more weeks. Your body has swallowed your sugars and fats, now it's turning to your muscles, then it will swallow your brain and heart. One of your teachers I spoke with said you have gifts. That you perceive things with originality. That ideas excite you. Affirm this by eating. Nothing is improved by throwing yourself away. Nothing in this town is made better by your death. If you eat, you will be here for a few years, the town requires that as recompense, but then you could be free to live how you like and argue for what you believe in. You are twenty-two? Is that right? You're just beginning. Let this be a chapter in a worthy life." He points at the tray. "Make use of this. Make use of the life you have."

"If you want that tray to be useful," says Babello, "walk with it across town, and cross the river. When you get behind the last street of homes, keep climbing, and you'll find my friends, living in tents. Bring it to them with your benevolence."

"You know about them?"

"That's my family."

"Impossible! You've lived here your whole life. I know that."

"I collected their stories into a book."

"That's impossible too! I've read every book, save for thirteen."

"It's a collection of some portraits and the conversations of people whom you have had no interest in knowing."

"There's no such thing. It would be in the library if it existed."

"Why would I contribute to your library?"

"But I want to read it!"

"Not everything people make is for you."

"But it's knowledge! Knowledge is for people!"

"You wrote to the mayor so you could join her and know her. Why didn't you think to know people before applying your systems to us? Why was it her you wanted to know and not the people of the town? There was a party I was at. One of your books went around the room and people read out parts and laughed at how naive you are."

Bhara twitches. With the row of bars between them, they stand before each other, until the mayor's chief aide turns. His feet slam on the sloped stones of the old stairs.

Without Bhara, the basement feels enlarged again, as though it's reverted to its usual proportions.

"You don't like my polemics?"

"I prefer conversation." The boy leans back against his workbench. "But it's my own fault. I've never had a headstrong friend before. I didn't know what you people are like. But Bhara's a madman. Equally polemical. You should never make him feel bad for not knowing things. It makes him vengeful. You'll have to make it up to him. He's the one you should be flattering, Bello. He's the one who can be lenient to you."

"I don't want lenience. I don't want favours. I don't accept his power. I won't submit to it."

"You use the bathwater that's brought to you. You wash with it every morning they bring it to you. How is that different from eating their meals? Why accept the goodwill of bathwater but not the goodwill of meals?"

Babello looks at the spot on the floor where the bucket is left for him.

"Will you stop bathing?" The boy waits, but Babello says nothing. "Besides, Bhara's right. You could get out of here and do anything you wanted! You could get married. Or go fishing. Or run for mayor. Just say the things that make Bhara happy."

§

At his bench, the boy works without apparent labour. His arms surrender to the habits of his task. He doesn't look up from his work; his hands simply seize the chisel or hammer from the tabletop. He only notices the passage of time when his stomach rumbles or when he steps aside and sneezes from the dust.

"Bello?" he asks without turning. "Can I ask you a question?"

"Sure."

"So, you won't eat meat?"

"No."

"Because it makes your body a graveyard for animals?"

He nods.

"So how come you don't mind being a graveyard for peas and carrots? Why is it perfectly fine to be a graveyard for a carrot and not a fish? How come…" the boy asks, beginning to smile, because Babello is smiling now, "wait, honestly, just wait, how come it is one thing to be a cemetery for chicken and fish and another thing to be cemetery for corn and bread?"

"Is that question real?"

"Of course it's real. Everything's real. My friend Vullie says even his fantasies are real."

"Where are you from? Surely you're not from this town if you're asking a question like that."

§

The boy works through the afternoon before wiping his face with his sleeve. He eats a pear he quartered and brought down in a bowl and covered with a cloth. "Bello," he says, breaking a silence between them, "never say anything bad to me about Giulietta. Don't even tell me one of her scandals. She's very instructive, Bello." The boy clears his desk and drops three pencils into the corner glass jar. "There's something very sincere and attractive about that. You know how most people, when you say hello, they smile and say hello back? Giulietta, though, when I say hello to her, she would kick my shins and pour honey over my head."

"Sincerity is rare."

"She dislikes me so much." The boy shakes his head. "I have to admire that."

"Mazzu?"

The boy shakes dust from his shirt then faces Babello. "Yes?"

"Who's Giulietta?"

"Giulietta, Bello! I've told you. We've talked about her. She's the one I brought the mangos to. You know, you're very self-absorbed." He waves his arm. "You altruists are all the same." Shaking his head, the boy sweeps up the mess, hangs the broom from a nail, then turns to leave the basement with the last wedge of pear. Up, in the kitchen, he fills two glasses of water and carries them back downstairs.

§

The first evenings Giulietta was visited by Mazzu, she was surprised by how at ease she felt. She took pleasure in explaining the history of whatever object he pointed out from the windowsill—a brush, a painting, a pair of slippers. The boy listened and drew a line between gifts given to her and those things she chose for herself. He was able later to discern between the two sets, so that after twelve nights' conversations he felt he understood her taste, her path through her fifteen years, and he could anticipate the last words to some of her phrases. He joined her, completing some sentences as her own lips discovered what words she would use. He burst into her life and then, with the last two nights having passed without a visit, she found herself missing his attention and manner.

In the rosy dreams of her adolescent mind, what Giulietta once imagined for herself were nights of glamour. A lively life with a tug of war between countless friends. This was initially barred by her parents' strict code, then, as she aged, by the stubborn solitude that she helped author. Sitting on her bed to tuck her in, her parents made her promise to carry nothing precious when she walked through the town, to keep her eyes averted, and avoid acting out because of her pride or temper. They were certain that the peak of breeding and behaviour was within homes, not outside of them. Beyond their walls were barbarism, indolence, and brutality. When she did go out, it was with an extreme vigilance that overcharged her nerves and reflexes. So, with the bulk of her time spent studying the paintings her parents bought, practising music, or staring from her second-storey window, the town that she pieced together from others' impressions was imaginary.

Giulietta is in her bedroom and hears her mother call her for dinner. What can she do to revive his visits? What he has done is reveal the crisis of her life: that her days and conversations have little substance. How had this been revealed in just a few evenings of conversation? It's absurd, she declares to her mirror as her mother calls her again.

What is it we love in another? Is it something so tangible it can be shaken out into language and perspective? Giulietta used to envision liking someone gallant, someone with solemnity and an honourable bearing. But Mazzu seems to be a member of an earthier breed. With his lightness and bombast, she is sure he will never need her. He will never even permit himself the depth of desperation she used to think was the essential sign of love. With her mother's cries for dinner flying through the house, Giulietta stops in the hallway outside the kitchen and the noise of her family beginning to eat. She pushes her hand through her hair, her right elbow high for several moments, then goes back to her bedroom and shuts the door.

What if everything she knows is wrong? What if loving someone has nothing to do with despair or agony or trials? What if it is closer to a carnival, something to be measured more by laughter than by tears? And those paintings she cherishes? Are they false? And their secret symbols and signs—what if there are no big symbols? Only big idiots? Feeling as though Gaspo has tricked her with a counterfeit melancholy, she glares at the dresser drawer that holds the leather-bound book. Her eyes fix on it, as if burning the imposter. Giulietta goes over to the window, catches a reflection of herself, and stares through it to the town beyond. What she wants is to bump casually into Mazzu and fling aside her pretensions. She peers down the hallway. She closes the bedroom door and, standing in the safety of her room, Giulietta jumps into the air. She smooths her hair and dress back into place and takes a deep breath. She goes down toward the kitchen. Stopping in the hall again just before the final corner, she jumps again, higher this time, her ankles springing her weight. She spends dinner battling to suppress a smile. She passes the salad bowl, the pot of chili flakes, the wooden-handled bread knife to her family with unusual glee.

§

In the sanctum of his single-floor home, with the pruned plants and orderly kitchen, Bhara stops pacing. Each day as he comes into his office, he pauses to scan the house for unnecessary sounds. Even the unlatched gate and its wood banging with the wind against the frame could disrupt his thinking. Or wind churning through the giant leaves of his neighbour's tree—those huge leaves brushed against his wall—even that intrusion roused him from the depths of oceanic thought.

"It is absurd that I went and visited him! Absurd that I didn't know about his book." Standing in the small room, Bhara shakes his head, raises his chin, and contemplates the law.

How many years has he spent hammering his mind into an instrument: a silver, glinting needle, capable of debate or vigorous written discourse, only to have some aberration bloom in front of him? Bhara resumes pacing, unable to sit, irritated with himself, irritated by his lack of discipline, and irritated by something more. "Absurd," he mutters, "that I went there and showed them my incomplete knowledge."

He worked his mind, and it has failed him. It matters because he represents the law. He is its upholder, an embodiment of its perfection and objectivity. If he is imbued with concessions and exceptions, then the law too is marred by these divots. So, it matters. He has hammered his mind into severity and it has failed him. And they each saw that, Babello and the boy. He has imbued the law with the frailty that comes from improvisation and let them gape at it. He shakes his head.

With the humiliation of his morning's prison visit overshadowing him, Bhara leaves the room. It is hours before Katrina will be home. She will understand. She has such faith in him.

Bhara walks across town toward a favourite park bench. He sits in the shade beneath a lopsided tree and gazes around. Some children kick a ball. Two others bicycle down a grassy hill.

This was only a minor error, he reassesses. He will make others, but will surmount them as he has surmounted everything. He will find that elusive book and rededicate himself to his intellectual completion. Perhaps he is not the sole embodiment of the law after all, so his humbling of it was less severe than he thought. The town's laws are beyond him, above him, beautiful, pure, abstract, immune to his touch and fallibility. If Babello and Mazzu could not see it, that was because of their weakness. It was merely he who was diminished, and now, by pulling the weed from the soil, the garden was saved. He had overcome it.

Bhara rises. He looks around. A couple of leaves flutter down. To think that all the order and harmony and growth he sees is enabled by the town's simple booklet, *Sixteen Laws*! Every relationship and comfort flourished because of the reciprocity of clear rules! These mechanisms soften his heart. How subtle, he thinks, and essential these structures are! How they extract what is best in people! And to think how that little handful of paragraphs knits everyone into such a diverse coexistence.

He will make Katrina a fine dinner. He has overcome his error. Bhara crosses through the park in his long strides. His mind, a silver, glinting needle, could tear through rock. The morning's absurdity diminishes nothing, because he has overcome it. He wants coriander and tomatoes. By necessity, he is alone with his griefs and elations—it has to be this way; he has ventured so far intellectually. He will handle the wet coriander gently. He will subdue his excitement and be attentive to Katrina. He could get wine, and afterward they will walk it off. Katrina humbles him, riding those waves that cuff his island and break over his stones, with her devotion and clarity, without reprimand for his aloofness and solitude, without complaint. She loves him. And afterward they can walk off the wine.

§

Bhara pushes into the afternoon market and edges his way toward the vegetable sellers, who toss the bruised pieces into hobbled wagons behind them. Spotting Mazzu in a yellow shirt walking alongside another boy, who pushes a bike, Bhara holds up his arm and yells for him.

Hearing that name, Giulietta stops and turns around too. She presses toward that raised arm.

Bhara pulls a folded sheet from his breast pocket. "This is a list of seeds you may want to try in that trough. They are in order from the least expensive to the most. I drew it up quickly, but it should help. This one should grow the quickest in that light. I'm sorry for coming to speak with Babello," Bhara says, changing tone.

The boy looks up at Bhara. "It was important what you said to him. It was intelligent. He should hear that. Believe me: I've asked him to eat too."

He doesn't see the significance, Bhara thinks. "Do you talk to him?"

"Oh, yes. Bello and I have long talks now."

"What about?"

"The usual things. Love. Truth."

"Love?" Bhara asks.

"I believe him," Vullie says. "This one's a madman for love. We've been carrying a ladder back and forth across town all week, trying to find it."

"You're one of the mail carriers? You're Vullie?"

"Absolutely."

"Have you heard of someone carrying mail beyond the river to the settlement there?"

"That's me. I do that. We even made a postal station out there."

"Vullie just asked for a box," Mazzu adds.

"It's just a box with shelves for now, but I have plans. I want it to be like the other postal stations, with a tea stand and water and two benches for talking and reading the papers."

"You know you're not supposed to deliver there. Our stamps don't cover any area west of the river. You should stay within the boundary."

"I don't take stamps for those deliveries."

"What? How long has this been happening?"

"A week or two. I don't know."

"Is this why the deliveries for the mayor are coming late in the day? Because you're having to go all that way and back? The mayor gets priority."

"My deputy has been special-delivering the mayor's mail every day."

"You know that there is a rule that these people have to register in the town before they can receive town services such as mail?"

"See, that's when I started doing it. I thought, they need to know this rule. They hadn't even heard of it. I even collect the newspapers I find and bring them to the stand for the people to read."

"But they're not staying there. Mail is for permanent addresses. They don't have an address."

"I always manage it just fine. Everything gets in the right hands. Besides, Mazzu often reminds me nothing here is truly permanent. You shouldn't worry so much. I have it worked out. Besides, if it gets complicated, I can make up street names."

"Street names need to be registered! No one can just make them up."

"We made a name for the post office there. Mazzu gave the name for it. Mazzu called it WoW. West of West. And you know what happened? I put up a sign saying 'wow.' And now *wow* is their slang for mail. Isn't that wonderful? 'Where's the wow?'" Vullie turns to Mazzu. "Aren't they wonderful? We should go back and have dinner there again. Mazzu likes their drumming. But his courtship has eaten into our fun nights."

As the two boys turn away from Bhara, they face Giulietta. Her eyes are large and giddy. The boy is off-balance and unable to find a thing to say.

Smiling and facing him and unable to find words herself, she jumps into the air. Giulietta jumps a second time. Then a third. Vullie looks over at Mazzu. Mazzu watches the girl jump a fourth, fifth, and sixth time, her ankles springing her up and her dress puffing in the air and her hair rising. Without knowing why, Mazzu jumps too.

"Tonight, I want my mango," Giulietta says.

"That's obvious now," Mazzu says.

"It is?"

"Each of us here, hopping together in a market."

Passing children stop, gather, and leap into the air. "Vullie," says Mazzu, "nothing you could have said today could have prepared me for this!" Surrounded by hopping children, Vullie joins them and springs up casually into the air.

§

Babello reaches between the bars. He touches the trough and handfuls of the earth and massages clumps apart. He sprinkles earth over the tray of food. The smell of the soil rises into the air and hangs on his hand so later he wears the scent like a glove. He sits on the mattress, elbows on his knees, then on the floor, leaning against the wall. With hunger grinding in him and exacerbating his thoughts, he gazes out of the barred window. He imagines his friends and Isabella, and wonders what their days are like and what they may be talking about. *No, it's only been two weeks*, he thinks. *Nothing will have changed. It'll all be the same*. Babello wills himself to pace the basement cell, wishing the boy were here. His company is an axe, splitting Babello from the lure of the meal tray. When he hears a noise or skittering sound, Babello glances over, hoping to see the boy hop down the stairs and resume their flippant patter. He walks over the cell floor, which is splitting and becoming grassy, and he gazes through the window at the garden and the wind that blows over the hilltop, flattening the grass.

§

In the town's evening marketplace, the boy takes the list that Bhara wrote and hands the page to a seed vendor. The boy points to the list's top entry. "Do you have the one with the star beside it?"

The vendor nods, confused by the discrepancy between the systematic list and the boy who pulls only a few coins from his loose shirt pocket. The vendor asks the boy how many he needs. Mazzu shrugs and tries to think of how many bars make the cell's breadth. "Maybe twelve?" The man scoops at the bag of seeds and pours them into the boy's breast pocket. He refuses the coins and gives a lesson in how to plant the seeds. In the ground behind his chair, the vendor draws a furrow with his heel then mimes dusting soil over it.

In the basement, the boy follows this example. He digs a furrow with one hand and drops the seeds one by one along the length of the trough and covers them. Upstairs, he fills a container with water and pours it over the soil. He waits. "Look. It doesn't leak, Bello." Mazzu waits there, holding the container. "Bhara's obsessive. These should grow, shouldn't they? With anyone else, I would have less hope, but with Bhara—I think he picked ones that will grow. Look, there's still no water leaking. Do you think it will take weeks or months?"

"For what, Mazzu?"

"For these vines to grow. I got the best seeds. Someone just gave them to me. You're not listening to me?"

§

In Giulietta's backyard garden, there is a ladder between Mazzu and Vullie, and on the grass there is a watermelon.

"I don't think I thought this through, Vullie. How do I get that up the ladder?"

"What was your plan?"

"I think I'm just going to go up anyway," Mazzu shrugs. "Let's see what she says." He climbs the rungs and taps on her window.

She pokes her head out the window. She holds her hair back as she leans out. "No gift today?" She is still in the dress she wore at the market. Mazzu liked the printed triangles.

"There is a watermelon," the boy says, pointing to the grass. Vullie waves up.

"How come it's down there?"

"It's the same, really," Mazzu says. "Down there, up here, really there is little difference. It's still for you." Giulietta pulls him in by the shoulders. She leans past him and shuts the window, then sits and pats the bedspread.

Nervous to be so near her, the boy quietly complies. He sits beside her, silent and unsure.

She looks at his hands. She lifts his sleeve to see his arms. She puts her hand against his. Though his fingers are longer, hers are more slender and appealing. She traces his fingers and hand. She feels his forearm and measures it against her own, paler, narrower arm.

"What do you do when you're not with me? What were you doing before you came to me?"

"Talking."

"With who?"

"A man I've met," the boy says without thinking. "A criminal. Beside where I work, there's a cell."

"You work?"

She looks at his other hand and opens it. His nails aren't cut evenly, and there are calluses at the base of his fingers.

"I used to work alone. I'd be alone most of the day. But now he's always beside me. He's always there."

"Does he bother you?"

"Only when we first met."

"Is he angry?"

"He was, but I can feel him reconciling."

"What does he say?"

The boy sifts through the conversations he's had with Babello while she holds his hands and sets them on her knees. "He said...he said we must each do a beautiful thing. In our life, we must do something beautiful. He thinks I'm rich."

"Are you?"

"I'm nothing. My house is bigger than this, but it isn't mine."

"What's in your bedroom?"

"Come one day. I can show you."

"It's too far. I couldn't get there safely."

"It's not much farther than the market. You just have to climb the hill."

"When I go out, if I linger, or get caught up, I come home and my mother is scared at the front door. My father was robbed twice. They were brave after the first time, but the second time changed them."

"It happens. They shouldn't worry so much."

"They make me dress differently when I go out. So people think I have nothing. My mum thinks if I wear strings on my wrists people will think, look, that girl can't even afford jewellery. She saw girls wearing string bracelets and thought that could mislead people and protect me. That's why I wear dresses like this."

"Were you allowed out before the drought?"

"Only with my parents. Tell me about your house and room. What's in it?"

"Come down the ladder and climb back later in the night. Vullie will help."

"Describe your room to me."

"There's a tree outside my window."

She imagines the window centred on the wall, instead of how it is, off to one side and narrow. "And in your room?"

"My bed. And my desk."

"See, you have something. Those are yours."

"They were given to me."

"That makes them yours."

"It doesn't feel that way."

"The man in the cell, what was his beautiful act?"

"A fire."

"I like fires too. I lose myself when I watch them, and everything that bothers me goes away, and I feel like things don't matter. I have a tin that I used to light fires in, but my parents found out even though I did it near my window."

The boy nods. "Me too. I did that too. But Papa caught me."

"Was she mad?"

"No. She said it was normal to be fascinated. But she didn't want me to do it in the bedroom. So we played with it in the basement, where it's all stone. I liked putting different types of bark in and watching them catch. Then, when I had enough, we threw water over it all."

"Is the prisoner trying to win you over?"

"No. He doesn't even know my parents died in a fire."

"How didn't he know that?"

"But without that fire, I wouldn't have what I have now. I wouldn't have Papa. I wouldn't have my workshop, or my room, or all the things I've made. And I wouldn't be known by people. All I would have that I have now is Vullie." The boy's mind shifts. "I don't know what the prisoner does all day. He just looks out of the window. There isn't anything to see. I went to the back garden and stood under his window to see what he sees. There isn't anything to look at. And he spends his days staring at it."

"One poet says if people are melancholy they're not really looking. They look anywhere and all they see is themselves."

"That's Zuraffi. She's my poet."

"I think a person's unhappiness is so deep that they can stare into it for hours and only begin to fathom it." She brings Mazzu's hands to her knees and then to her cheek. "Do you get that way?"

"Yes."

"But you hide it?"

"Yes."

"Why?"

"It's shameful."

"It isn't."

"I don't want people to know it about me."

"Melancholy is beautiful. It shows a mind that isn't typical."

Entranced by her, the boy still shakes his head. "No. It shows a mind so weak it can't solve its problems. Besides, the prisoner isn't always melancholy. We joke too. Sometimes he gets lighter because he believes he's going to win."

"What could he win?"

"The battle with Bhara."

"Who's Bhara?" she whispers, with his hand still against her cheek, then her collar. "Tell me about all these people."

"Come down the ladder with me."

"I can't."

"Just come down and then come back up."

"I've never even been on a ladder."

"It's no different from stairs, except you even have something for your hands to hold."

She uses a picture frame to prop her window open. The ladder shakes with her steps. "Slowly," the boy says. She looks down at the dark yard. Mazzu follows after her.

Vullie takes a switchblade and carves up the watermelon, and the three of them sit on the grass and eat it.

On her way back up, she stops a few rungs above them and looks down. "I think this is the most fun I've ever had." She takes the picture frame from her window and eases the window closed.

§

On the edge of town, five men lift a heavily loaded cart and run with it. Setting it down around a corner, they knife through the cover and dive into the merchandise. They carry away heads of lettuce, paper cones of almonds, fruits. One man holds four corners of a fabric and fills it as if it were a sack, running with it bouncing over his shoulder. Within an hour, the cart of produce is bare.

And one morning a merchant returns from his lunch and finds his storefront blasphemed. When the straw-hatted merchant turns to passersby with his arms out and his son hiding behind his leg, instead of consolation, he receives taunts. This isn't just, the merchant says, shielding his child. Other merchants, facing similar threats and brazen acts, release the contents of their stores without receiving any payment.

Petty crime sinks its teeth into the edges of Baraffo.

On the western outskirts, the settlement of tents multiplies. The farmers and the children of the farmers walk in from the parched lands and join the encampment in this plain that rises into the mountains. Day after day, the tents, built with knotted cloths and propped up by planks and branches, spread into the foothills. Papa leads Bhara across the town to the encampment. They duck under laundry lines. Branches hammered into the ground fence in chickens. Papa smiles at the residents and promises to supplement their livestock. She hands out fishing nets. Bhara follows Papa around, irrelevant beside the garrulous mayor.

§

Late that night, in the mayor's house, Mazzu walks into the basement with a lamp swinging from his hand. "You want me to fill up your glass?"

Babello brings it to Mazzu from the windowsill.

"Have you been brooding about Bhara and his speech, Bello?"

Seeking a distraction from the hunger that prevented him from sleeping, Babello points to the deck of cards. So the boy sets the lamp on his stool and they sit on the floor and play.

"Explain this again," Mazzu says, indicating the tray. "I don't understand. How does not eating make you stronger?"

Taking the cards that Babello passes between the bars, Mazzu receives his subversive education.

Knowing how the parables he used in their first conversation repelled the boy, Babello tries another approach. "There was an argument in class one day. It was all over a single word. It was a fight a classmate took up with our history teacher. She wanted to have a word changed, from *nomad* to *dispossessed*. Our teacher argued with her, proudly citing the exact definition of *nomad*. Just like Bhara, he said he appreciated her, but then derided their dispute as worthless and without impact. One night, we were all talking at our house when she decided how to crack his stance apart. What she did was arrive each day a little thinner. She came to our classes until she walked like a ghost in her exaggerated clothing. During her hunger strike, she never missed a class. She took notes and would meet his eyes with self-respect. In just the second week, she broke him. He was scolded by his supervisors and he came one day and apologized. That day of his apology was when he looked most human. And she did that so simply. She changed how that class will be taught. She made that class more honest."

"Isabella was there too?"

"Yes. Of course. We were all meeting in our home."

"Who did she agree with? It's a quibbly change, Bello. Does it really matter? Especially if you all know the truth anyway. It doesn't change life. It's a thing that only seems like a victory if you're small."

"You can't let this terminology become entrenched. If you do, it gains force. If they pile high enough, they naturalize into truths and then into laws, and then entire families can be ruined without a thought." Babello arranges his cards. "Besides, if it was inconsequential, why would the teacher have been so set against it?"

"His pride, Bello. He didn't want to go back on himself after he said it out loud to a roomful of students."

"No, she enlightened him."

"And you want to enlighten Bhara?"

"You're not willing to see it yet, but this town isn't adequate. In some years, you'll see it. Then you'll have to decide to act on what you see or ignore it and live as others do, without being fully human."

"Papa's good. She's a good person. I know her."

"Then you have to explain to me why life in this town isn't more fair. Please. Explain that to me. How is she good and the town unfair?"

"You won't eat? You ate on the first day."

"I wasn't thinking then. I was worked up."

"Isabella didn't agree with the woman, did she? With her hunger strike?" The boy smiles. "I knew that, Bello. I could tell."

"She always thinks we shouldn't embarrass others. She thought our teacher was humiliated for not being perfect or for just expressing the thoughts of his time. She wanted the conversation to happen in private. She knew his family. But she did think he was wrong."

Hearing a scuttling over the floor, the boy freezes. He hears it again, the sound of stone being scratched. He peers over the far end of the trough and recoils. He flings his water that way. He throws a scrap of wood. The block bangs off the tray. Babello leaps up too. He sees the eyes of the swarming rats and their burbling movement. They scatter from the circle of light as the boy lunges with the lamp. Mazzu surges around the basement, the lamp turned up to the brightest pitch, shining it at the walls and corners. "I hate rats, Bello," he yells. "I've heard that for every rat you see there are actually seven. Bello, just yell anything. They hate noise." With any twitch of noise or movement, Mazzu lunges toward that area. "Are you afraid of rats?" he asks, raising the lamp. Babello stands, holding the bars. He raises his arm to his eyes. "Just sing something then while I'm gone," Mazzu says, leaving the lamp by Babello's feet. With the boy upstairs searching for soap and a bucket of water, Babello holds a bar as his eyes sweep the floor.

§

Noticing Bhara has stayed late, Mazzu knocks on a door in the upstairs hallway and walks into the library. Bhara sits with a box of papers in his lap. "Bhara, I know you have principles and Bello has principles, but rats are coming into the basement. He won't eat the food. I've heard him. He's definite. Ask the guards, tell them to stop bringing the trays. It's useless."

Bhara shuts his eyes.

"He won't eat. I promise you. I asked him. He means what he says."

"Is his dinner down there now?"

"I just threw it away. But there were many rats. They made a mess. It's where I work."

"I'll talk to someone. We won't leave the trays overnight again. Mazzu?" Bhara calls. The boy turns back. "When you and Babello talked about love, what is it he said?"

"You should ask him yourself. Give yourself time, though. What you can do is make an afternoon of it."

"It doesn't concern me, but—Mazzu? If you pull an ulterior motive from him, can you tell me?"

"Bhara, are you listening? What hidden motive could there be? He's giving up his love to be locked in here. He believes in what he's done. He's proud of it. He's not hotheaded. He thinks what he's done is just, and he has conviction."

"But he talks about love?"

"Bhara, when him and Isabella are together, even the bedsheets pant. The paint blushes and flees the walls. The pillows, they flip upside down to hide their eyes! Just be near him and you'll sense it. Just don't bring him more food. He's made his decision. You won't persuade him."

§

Mazzu crosses the basement. The boy sweeps up the crumbs then splashes a couple pails of foamy water out over the floor. He leaves the lamp there on the stool overnight, but tells Babello to shut it off when he feels secure. "I don't want them coming back either," the boy says. "But it should be fine now. They won't like the smell of that soap. They'll find it off-putting and scurry away somewhere else." The boy waves a goodnight and climbs up to his bedroom.

§

In the dark, Bhara walks across town. He opens his front door and rinses his face with warm water, undresses without disturbing his wife, and slips into bed. He lies like that, trying to sleep, before a surge of doubt drives him into the hallway. Even in her sleep, Katrina senses his absence. She waits, then ties her robe on and finds him in the garden. He pulls her onto his lap and plays with the tassels on her robe.

"What is it?"

"Papa and I walked over to visit those living in the tents. There are ninety-seven tents now. They haven't even recited *Sixteen Laws*. What obliges us to them? It's in the laws themselves: if they don't recognize the laws, the town doesn't recognize them. Why do they refuse to say them? I followed Papa around and counted the people. We had soup and bread with them. But they wouldn't even look at me. None of them. They hate me. They revile me. And why?"

"You don't have flaws people can love. You're so perfect. Look at the mayor: her limits are right there for people to feel kinship with. But she needs you now. You offered to help. So, give her what you have. You'll have time for your other things after you help Papa through this tension. But don't quit. The town isn't safe. People don't trust each other. Wait until this passes, and then you can speak with Papa and tell her. Now, come back to bed."

§

Images of Babello proliferate. His portraits are pinned to posts and walls, and the song that the boy lofted into the basement air has become an anthem, a shorthand for a whole political movement. The boy sits in the basement wind wearing a sweater, absorbing neither the image nor the song, but the origin, whose talking interweaves with his hunger. Mazzu brings news of the evolving town into the basement; Babello listens and interprets.

"This town will erupt soon," Babello says.

"No, you're exaggerating what I said. Most are fearful. They don't know you or look to you. You're just a curiosity and something for people to speculate about. It's like when there was a white butterfly and people followed it around and said where they'd spotted it."

§

"I have 275."

"I can't remember what I have."

"You have 310. Bello, I need the ten of spades. Are you hoarding the ten of spades?"

In the basement of the mayor's home, with the town cloaked in blackness, the lamp that's perched atop the boy's stool spreads its glow over their cards. Mazzu's orange sweater is wide across his shoulders and the sleeves are long for him, so he folds them up. It bulks over his wrists.

"You think Papa is rich, don't you?"

"Of course she is."

"But this is all only a loan," Mazzu says. "When someone else is elected, where do Papa and I go? She doesn't have another house."

"Being rich and having power are the same thing. It's about having choices. She could get a home anywhere. She will be welcomed and helped. No one would obstruct her. That is wealth. You're inheriting that."

"What is it, Bello? What's wrong with you tonight?"

"More than any crime," Babello says, with a hand over his eyes. "More than the fire, what I am guilty of is hatred. I've hated this town, and these people. I've hated the good things people have that make them want to keep this town just as it is, instead of reforming it. I hate their meals and furniture, and the politeness that makes it seem like the difference is fine." He puts his cards down. "Just leave me tonight."

With his head down, Babello leans into the window as rancour overtakes him. He squeezes the bars. Upstairs, Mazzu pulls the bed sheet over his shoulders, then he removes his sweater, throwing it on the floor before falling into needed sleep.

8

The people of Baraffo had traditions to quell the habitual late-summer rains. Assuming that all things in their cosmos were personal, one mother, generations ago, rose to her feet during the summer rain. "It is childish. The sky is simply being childish." She drew her friends from her home and coaxed them to defy the rain and stare up at the sky. She was sure that the clouds, abashed by their long stare, would become disciplined and hold off their spate. Another woman plunged the knife she was cooking with into her waterlogged lawn. By the time she came back and pinned the door closed behind her, the rumour of her solution had rippled through the town, and kitchen knives filled the town's grass. By the morning, their wooden handles eroded with the night's water, slid off the metal, and bobbed toward the sea. Baraffo's usual summer deluge would continue, tugging wheelbarrows, horses, and sheds downstream. The fish wandered from the riverbed into the knee-high water of the roads, swimming with giddy liberty. Some men, prone to regret and soul-searching, pointed at the fish with self-reproach.

"Their years of ascetic river life have paid off," these men said. "Look at them, prospering, rubbing their freedom in our faces." But, each year, nearing the end of the summer, the rain would give in to the power of the town's customs and abate, Baraffo would bake, the knives that were lodged in the lawns rusted and flaked, and the town was restored.

The people of Baraffo could perform these actions to lead them through the summer deluge, but they had no methods or rituals when they encountered a stretch of weeks so parched that only once did the people of Baraffo experience rain.

During the drought's single shower, the people of the town stood outside with their arms raised. "Where have you been?" some asked. "This is inadequate," they said after that one night of rain, and endured a further five weeks' thirst while decrying the sky as petulant, fickle, and cruel. On some streets, the word *sky* became a pejorative; it was hardly spoken. Some wondered if their firmament had itself died and left them in a merely physical world, without any signs or purpose. They lifted their chins and stared up at the blue. "Please," they pled. "Please rain."

"We have been forsaken," they lamented.

"We are being left behind," they said.

"We are being forgotten. We are being abandoned," they said, pulling up uselessly dry plants. "We are being sacrificed…"

The summer of drought. Throats and soil ached for relief. The grass withered into straw and broke underfoot so trails of footprints were left across fields. A gust of wind tugged plants from their soil and blew leaves over roads. Stronger gusts uprooted hedges or small trees. One person, trying to cross a street grabbed the elbow of a stranger, who in turn took hold of the elbow of another, the three of them ducking together as liberated gardens passed overhead.

With the stress of the drought, social fissures hardened into grudges. Families fractured, friends feuded, and rivals brawled.

The farmers north of the town, who were sick of seeing their crops crumble in the breeze, bought tins of green paint and spread them over the soil. In the evenings, they drank together, moving as a crowd from house to house, praising each other's illusory crops. When they had visited all of the farms, they went loudly into town. On waking the next morning, they found fruits and meat that, on witnessing their convivial community, must have jumped into their pockets and followed them home. The merchants closed their ransacked stalls and complained to the mayor. "There is a discrepancy," they argued in response to the mayor's words, pushing their tone of irritation to the permissible limit, "between each night's contents and our morning's inventory. Each day there is this discrepancy. We are being robbed." One man who was present at this meeting persuaded Papa to employ the farmers as labourers to build a jail. The mayor conceded, reassured the merchants, and sent them away. Placated, they reopened their stalls.

In converting Baraffo's horse stables into a general jail, the farmers worked with characteristic zeal. If the craftsman whom the mayor asked to design the prison sneezed, his pencil's steady line hiccupping on the page, he would leap up and see that the men had already completed that new section of wall with deft, curving brickwork. The farmers stood in front of him, in uneven rows, smiling and raising their eyebrows, despite their hunger, while they awaited the craftsman's next tentative idea.

After the first month of drought, the people of the town turned on each other. Certain that their town's general sinfulness had invited the disaster, some opted to wear only white and hurried around condemning the prodigals and yelled for moral conduct to be the mission of each day. These white-shirted ones complained about the town's customs, before tempering their condemnations when seeds of sin were found within themselves.

In the second month of drought, the wood of the houses moaned. Fruit hardened and became gemlike. Tributaries dried. People clambered down the bank, stood in the bed, and looked forward and back.

The drought stomped on. Townspeople shoved each other, competing over the buckets drawn from wells. And the make-shift tents at the western edge of Baraffo became a community. Its people wandered into town, searching for work and food. Pushed beyond the brink of what they could tolerate, the despairing people of Baraffo dove into the delusions of their imaginations and, veiled in their brightest colours, they walked the town with the bravery of optimism. Exiled from all comfort and security, these fabulous refugees admonished those who gave in even momentarily to dreariness or complaint or dared to lead conversations to something as upsetting as the solemnity of truthtelling.

For the duration of the drought, the people of Baraffo hid their fear from their children and grieved away from them. They tried to make their youth feel the future was certain and assured, that they would prosper, even while their own spines drooped.

This is becoming a desert, they whispered.

During that summer, the people of Baraffo stood before pieces of glass, studying their bodies. They ceased celebrating birthdays and recriminated their former days of abundance. They stood at the shore and watched the sea's salty excess wash over the stones. The waves came in, again and again. The people reviled that water. With each wave, they accused it of rudeness and flaunting.

They found the logic of their world unknowable. Crouching, longing for the return of their missing deity, they traced sacred shapes into the sand of their roads—triangles, flattened circles, limitless spirals that many people collaborated on—and walked by these symbols that the wind lifted into the air and blew over their darkened legs.

Want hollowed their minds, and these cavities became troughs for their blossoming incomprehension. Nothing was known. Nothing was certain. Nothing was sure or ordained. Friends embraced in disbelief; their skeletons met through their clothes. Why? they wondered. Why?

Toward the end of the drought's second month, the people of Baraffo felt themselves abandoned. They lamented their tribe, their collection of customs, their way of being, their tangled and unlit family histories. They painted the interiors of their homes with their personal sagas, fantastical depictions of their inner journeys that stretched from wall to wall. Why be here? Why be born? They uttered questions and felt that their suffering was fundamental. Why serve this term? We have been crushed before our greatness. We have dried before becoming wine. Our blood hasn't bred. We've been born into slaughter. They stood before their mirrors. Their shoulders were corded and their faces were startling.

Shaking and gaunt, they sheltered in each other and uttered oaths and vows. They slept with constant contact. Without much bread or fruit to eat, their skin sloped from their ribs to the narrowness of their bellies and out to their feet.

Throughout those months, the people of the town, tiptoed around the terms *famine, hunger, thirst*. They thought that voicing these terms would strengthen the weather's muscle and provoke the full fury evoked by these words. So, as in other matters (physical pain, crises, mortality), the people of Baraffo hid behind the shields of whimsy and sunniness, and used them to medicate unbearable grief.

Some of the people of the town, driven mad during the parched third month, took to the foothills and bayed their concern like pathological dogs. These guttural cries draped the town, covering Baraffo in inarticulate commentaries of grief, upsetting birds from the branches. Everyone else carried on with their life as best as they could, accompanied by dirges.

Those who once glutted themselves ate with thrift, and those who once ate with thrift starved. Crime became common. Guards were hired to patrol neighbourhoods and instructed to make an example of the thieves they caught. There were public beatings, but the hilltops were enclaves protected by barricades and governed by permissive rules.

In that third month, many of the citizens stiffened. Their elbows and necks and knees lost their fluidity, and their hair fell out.

At night, drummers roused their spirits.

Some people of the town uprooted themselves, bid farewell, and, without any destination in mind, ventured over the mountain or south along the treacherous coast, while those in the farmlands bid their own farewells and settled in Baraffo's foothills.

The seaside town strained.

The boy reads this history while he sits in the mayor's library. He scratches his head. He spent those months of drought absorbed in a project the mayor gave him: she wanted a system of birdfeeders to enhance the public garden behind the mayor's home. The boy had set to work on it, and every time he showed a drawing to the mayor, she urged him to dream of a structure that was more audacious, more inspired, one that would create a richness of song, so by the end, when the boy was questioning her judgment, it had taken three and a half months to build the assortment of oval entryways and chimes. Mazzu heard of the drought and knew they were in a period of rationing, but because of the challenge Papa gave him, the months passed by quickly and with little spare time. What he was led to believe was that the town was simply enduring a frugal phase that effected all equally. Sitting in the library chair, he envisions the difference in severity that he hadn't grasped.

§

After two weeks of his hunger strike, Babello's face is thin and his beard uneven. When he touches his face, it doesn't feel like his own. His short hair surprises him too. Babello turns from the window, his fingers still curled around the warm bars.

"What lines are you tapping, Mazzu? What poem are you carving today?"

The boy surfaces from his work. He has been focusing on the minutiae of each letter, trying to replicate each one without blemishes so they look standard, and so when the plaques are posted around town, the boy's hand will draw no attention away from Zuraffi's thoughts. The boy leans back and reads his handiwork with his unused morning voice. "'*Love* is a much abused word…'"

"'…and *beauty* no less so,'" Babello says, completing the line. "'I set fire to the courtesies of those terms.' She wants to be alone with everything, alone with the cliché of her imagination and her conventional heart. She wishes endearments existed only for her beloved. She wants those words entirely for herself, and for her own use. What is there to respect in that? What harm does it do anyone to let the words *beauty* and *love* be used freely?"

"It's a good sentiment," the boy whispers. "People overuse words that should be kept rare."

"In what kind of mind does love assume that tone? *She* is abusing the word *love*. Not us. Not people she derides for being unworthy. Why should *love* be rare? And tell me this. How come the love I feel never makes me want to limit the endearments of others? My love doesn't make me police the expression of others, whereas her love…what that poem…" Babello tries beginning his thought again. Mazzu watches Babello's aggravation, then looks at the lines he has carved within the grid of his pencilled hash marks.

Pushing the stool from the workbench, he picks up a page that blew to the floor. "How come you're angry today? Why are you worked up again? Breathe, Bello. It's okay…" The man's mood spreads throughout the basement, overshadowing the pleasure the boy derives from work. Mazzu picks up the chisel, then the piece of sandpaper. It takes some time before Babello's contagious mood recedes from the boy's mind and Mazzu loses himself again in the exactness of the craft.

Midway through the day, Mazzu turns on his stool. He looks at Babello, then at the floor, and notices the trays haven't stopped arriving. "You won't eat that, will you?"

"No."

"Why does the soil from the trough keep blowing out and over the tray? Is the wind doing that? I can take it away?"

"Yes."

"If you won't eat it, I won't leave it here."

A boiled egg has been added alongside the usual porridge. There are also pistachios that bump on the tray as the boy climbs the stairs. He throws the soil-covered egg away, but leaves the pistachios on the counter for others to graze on.

§

Throughout Baraffo, insinuations spread. The people of the town speak in undertones that hint at Papa's age and make inferences about her souring judgment and feel for the town. They wonder if they have extracted Papa's allotment of luck.

Wages sink. The owner of the town's Plum Building fires the workers who crowded there, assembling furniture and stitching clothes, and hires tent-dwellers at a cheaper wage. Those who were fired picket the building. At night, these newly unemployed are beside themselves with their own superfluity.

How could a person be excessive? they ask. We are too many, they say as their eyes survey the scene around them.

But, despite this misery, their epoch does feel significant. They can sense something: a new spirit warming at the margins.

With Babello pacing in the cell, some of them band together and climb over the new, eight-foot-high fencing around the Plum Building. They shove the hired guards. "We never had guards before," they yell. They jostle the guards, trample their hats, and the guards fight back.

The people of Baraffo watch the growing encampment on the edge of the town. They wonder if the prosperity of their town has peaked during their own lifetime. Foreboding darkens conversations. The people wait for Papa and wonder why she hasn't used her usual influence to maintain the town's equilibrium. "She is tired," they whisper.

"Her good run is finished."

"She is yesterday's mayor."

"And if her face can be brought low and rubbed in the dust, what will become of us?"

They walk alone and question the once indisputable magic of their life and feel it is no comedy, as they had once thought, but is instead a life of substantial woe.

When Bhara's name is mentioned, people spit on the ground, kick dirt over it, and grind it with their shoe.

Those close to the mayor counsel their neighbours, and they in turn counsel their ring of friends: "It would be wrong," they say, "to replace the mayor now."

"She has done so much for us."

"Let her serve out her term."

As this advice spreads through the town and meets the protests, there is suspicion that a loyal elite buttresses Papa.

§

Upstairs, the boy tiptoes into the mayor's bedroom and opens a desk drawer. He sifts through the keys and, going down the hallway, slips a silver one into a lock. In the library, he sits in the chair with a stack of pamphlets in his lap. With the door closed, he takes time to read through the green sheets, hunting for the history of the Peach Building, which Babello set on fire. Disregarding Bhara altogether, and finding the mayor preoccupied and Babello partisan, Mazzu believes that these documents are his most reliable tutor. In the library's armchair, flanked by dusty shelves, the boy absorbs a history. He learns about the two brothers, one who built and ruled the Peach Building with fury, and the more calculating brother who managed the Plum—each of the buildings named for the tint of its wood. He mulls the initial parables Babello told him. He has paraphrased them for Giulietta, and, sitting cross-legged on her bed, they unravelled the reasoning together. For Giulietta, personal safety preceded justice. Giulietta was also steadfast: vowing to comply with the *Sixteen Laws* is what made a person a dignified member of the town. The boy was more muddled, and unable to find a clear way of putting his thoughts.

§

It is evening when Bhara returns to the mayor's home. The boy and the mayor have both had their dinner.

"How is your pet project?" Mazzu asks, breezing by the chief aide in the hallway.

"My pet project?"

"Babello. And your studies of altruistic crime."

"He won't talk to me, Mazzu."

"He's very proud, Bhara. Very proud. He has more pride than the sun!"

"Why do you think the sun is proud?"

The boy looks at Bhara with a mystified expression. "Because it stays so far away."

"I spoke to him again today. I went downstairs when you were out. I thought that without you there, he would be more receptive. I only wanted to see if he wanted to do anything while he's in here. I had options for him. I've given him two tries now. I've been more than fair. The problem with Babello isn't just ideology, it's his mindset. He takes a bad situation and makes it worse. He's the opposite of you. You always make things better. I see what you've done in the kitchen, and the trough in the basement to grow vines. You're always improving things. Always productive."

On the carpet, standing between planters that bristle with branches and leaves, Mazzu shifts his weight from one leg to the other. "Babello wouldn't like to hear you speaking that way."

"No?"

"I just read about them. Anarchists can be very touchy about productivity."

"And it's such a shame."

"Maybe I can speak to him for you. We talk morning to night now. You shouldn't take it hard," the boy says. "He just thinks me worthy. Some like me more, others like you more." He shrugs. "I'm sure outside of dissident circles you are very popular."

Mazzu turns into the stairwell, drops down two flights, and enters the basement. He looks at the new tray of untouched food, sighs, and flings what remains of his glass of water at the trough. The boy assesses the progress the vines are making up the bars. Then he looks past that and at Babello, who sits in his roomy indigo clothes. Behind the vines, Babello lifts his head. His lips are white, and his neck is corded when he lifts his chin or turns to a side. In his hands, his veins are nets of blue.

"Bhara came to talk to me again. He's taken away my privileges. No more reading. No more bathing. He says that if I act better, I will be treated better."

"If you're willing to sit in jail without eating, what could he even offer you?"

"He says if I resume eating, I can write articles for the newspapers. He promised to have them published and he vowed that he wouldn't alter them."

The boy is impressed. "Wouldn't you like that?"

"Of course. But then I thought, what worth could it have if someone like Bhara concedes that to me? My hunger threatens him more than my opinion. He even brought me that tray himself," Babello says. "So, I think something must be happening. Something must be happening that's weakening his resolve." With his hands on the mattress and his arms straight, he shakes his head. "All day I've felt terrible."

"I can feel it from here. It's the hunger, Bello. You're just a dark cloud today. You'll just have to eat. There's nothing else.

I can even bring you something so the trays look untouched, so you can be doing the two things at once."

§

On the riverbank, Giulietta sits in the shade with a book of Zuraffi's writing that collects together early plays and poems. Giulietta has read through the book before, but it was a tepid experience that left her critical and gave her only a few phrases that she liked and copied down. Returning to it again confirms her earlier suspicions. There is something cold in her hands. Has Zuraffi even found anything worthy in life? And if she had, wouldn't she share it plainly and with the full force of personal style? Does she even find her life meaningful? Giulietta cannot identify even one belief that Zuraffi holds dear. Instead, there seems to be a void at her core that twins to her silence in the town. There is no mission, no gusting persuasion, no modelling of how to be. Instead of seasoning her writing with the wisdom of experiences, Zuraffi bases herself in a net of impersonal paradoxes that hold next to nothing. Where is the courage and openhearted belief? What is the point of all the invention if it lacks a certainty of spirit? Reading her, Giulietta feels a pointed question surging through her: Does Zuraffi know anything? Why would Mazzu laud something that's bloodless? Giulietta humbles herself, holds back her castigations, and carries that book with her for a couple days as she tries to see what has compelled the town to anoint Zuraffi its foremost poet.

Giulietta follows a path down to the water and climbs onto a stone. Looking to her left, she imagines the river's highland source, and to her right, the sea. The river weaves through the town without purpose, leaving islands where single trees reign. The sun is so bright that she can't even read out there. The opened pages overwhelm her eyes, so she walks downstream with her finger marking her spot in the closed book.

§

In the evening, the boy tidies his workbench. Mazzu drops the useful scrap wood into a pile to use another time. He brushes his table clean, sweeping dust and bits of wood into a pail. He unclamps the plaque he's finished and sets it onto the pile that he will varnish outside. "Bello," he announces, trying to cheer the prisoner's mood, "don't tell me anything bad about her! Don't even tell me one bad thing about Giulietta! Bello, even if her politics were stingy and her hair were like wires, still I would march across town to see her." Babello turns from the window and looks at the boy who sweeps the floor. "Even, Bello, if she lacked the ambition to parent her talents, still I could think fondly of her!"

"Even if her affection were marred by bombast?"

"Even so!" the boy says with triumph.

Midway up the stairwell, the bliss falls from Mazzu's face and he stops. He goes back down. "You're cagey. For an outspoken dissident, you're very cagey," Mazzu says to him, before going back up the stairs and gently tossing the mango between his hands as he walks out into the mellow evening light.

§

In an unlit bedroom, Mazzu and Giulietta whisper in the bed, on the yellow sheets of their enchantment. She looks at his hands and wants the story of a new scratch. Down the hall, her father hears something, ties his gown on, and knocks on her door. The boy hides behind the bed while Giulietta's father bends to kiss her cheek. As her father is about to go, he notices the window open, and the burgundy curtains lifting with the breeze.

Climbing back onto her bed, Mazzu is seized by an idea. "Have you been keeping the pits? You should be keeping all the pits," he whispers. "One day we will have a house. And we can plant all of the pits. The smell of our orchard would carry across town, toppling people from their bicycles." Giulietta undoes the necklace she wears. She lifts his hair and screws the clasps together behind his neck then pats it flat. "Are you listening? You should save all the pits," he whispers, lying back with her above him. "The smell of all the fruit trees would smother the town, and all of the bicyclists would topple over again and again, cursing Mazzu and Giulietta and their orchard of love."

"I want you to wear this everywhere you go. And if some-one teases you for wearing a woman's necklace, I want you to tell them, 'I am Giulietta's.'"

§

It's that night, well past midnight, when the mayor enters the basement with a lamp of her own. The boy freezes. He panics. Mazzu searches for excuses, but his mouth finds nothing. The lamp burns. The mayor kicks the trough and looks at the vines climbing the bars. She lifts her lamp and sees Babello, who squints with that face of his that has withered in the weeks of incarceration. "So? Am I the first?" she asks, breathing heavily.

Babello shields himself from the light. "No. Bhara's come twice. And the superintendent of the prison also came."

"Your brother is dead. Issan is dead. A second fire. The Plum Building this time." The mayor waits, standing above them. "He bettered you. He lay down and let the building burn down around him. People think this was heroic."

Soon after Papa leaves the basement, Bhara hurries in and repeats the same news. "What else will happen?" Bhara demands.

"I don't know anything."

"What else?"

"I know nothing," Babello says. Bhara races back up the stairs, using the wall to help speed him.

Left in the basement, the boy sits, needlessly holding the cards. Babello sits beside him with his face in his hands. They hear more steps thumping down the stairs without rhythm. Mazzu moves over to the stool to distance himself from Babello.

"Mazzu!" Vullie yells, turning into the basement. Vullie wipes his forehead, looks at the lamp, at the cards on the floor, at his friend, who's bewildered, then perceives the outline of another man deep in the cell. He pulls the boy by the shoulders and pushes him toward the stairwell. "Mazzu, there are riots. Someone died in a fire. Come on!" Vullie glances again, over his shoulder, and sees the silhouette move over to the window.

The boys run across Baraffo.

They wade through smoke and push through the gathering crowds. Groups lead chants of revolt. Together they witness an uprising. While they stand back, they see people tearing copies of the booklet *Sixteen Laws*. With the smoke rising, they watch the flames, then make their way around the Plum Building. Swift orange light shines on them. They listen to the fire's appetite. Their eyes tear up from the smoke. The wind pivots, blowing it away then blowing the foul air at them. They wipe their eyes and breathe shallowly, just sipping at the air to avoid coughing. Vullie pulls the collar of his shirt up and breathes through the filter of the cloth and motions for Mazzu to do the same. The boy pulls his shirt up over his nose. The two of them communicate with just their eyes or by pointing.

They stand near the burning Plum Building until dawn. When the sun rises, and with both of them weary, Vullie and Mazzu separate. The boy climbs the stairwell and crosses the lawn surrounding the mayor's home. His clothes heave with smoke. He searches the home and finds it empty. He cups water in his hands and blinks into these cool ponds, then winces with his eyes clenched shut and water running down his cheeks.

§

Babello's younger brother, Issan, lost his red cap climbing into the Plum Building. He climbed the scaffold and flipped himself in through a window he elbowed loose. He stood in the interior. When the fire took hold, he was walking with pride in the darkness. It was only when the flames brightened the interior into its spaciousness that Issan could move quickly. He ran to the far end of the building. He dropped halfway down a stairwell and swung himself over the rail, landing with both feet, thudding on the floor, but the main door he wanted to throw his body through was hazardous. He collected his breath with his hands on his knees, panting in the smoke. In the orange light, he scanned for better doors. He rushed up the stairwell, ran the length of the building, and dropped down another set of stairs. Issan was running on the main floor of the building, swallowing smoke, when a dislodged beam swung into him and swept him into the air. His body slammed against a pillar and he fell onto a workbench. He woke minutes later, soaking in the heat, his hand on his forehead, then he felt the pain, both hands diving for his leg. Ceiling beams crashed down. The large shells of lamps clanging around him too. Issan rocked back and forth on the tabletop, crying, bracing his broken leg. Another beam split from the ceiling's grip and pinned him. He tried rolling the weight off his chest. His lungs struggled to breathe against the impediment, his head flipping side to side like an animal caught in a trap it does not understand.

§

When Mazzu returns to the basement, he summarizes what he saw. In his spans of silence, as he presses a dripping towel to his eyes, he recalls more details and implications. He remembers the smoke piling in the sky, the ravenous sound of the flames as they chewed the building and fence around it, and all those who gathered to watch. "I don't understand what's happening," the boy says. With Babello leaning on the window ledge, his back turned, Mazzu receives no reply.

Mazzu trudges upstairs and, without removing his clothes or drawing the curtain or pulling his bedspread off, he flinches through a few hours of sleep.

At midday, with the fire still alive, Baraffo's air is acrid and dark, a horror to inhale. Smoke settles over a low-lying area. Those who live near the fire disperse to faraway homes.

§

Mazzu carries two empty glasses upstairs from the basement. After his scant sleep, he feels as if he lacks balance. He bumps against the walls and trips over a rug. In the kitchen, lifting the pitcher with both hands, he tilts the water out and overpours the glass. He rubs his eyes. His clothes are the same ones he wore to bed. Noticing the kettle, Mazzu stumbles over to it, but he brushes a bowl from the counter and misses as he lunges to catch it. The mayor hears the shatter.

When the kettle is whistling and the boy has revived enough to lift the wicker-wrapped handle, the mayor walks into the kitchen behind him. Her eyes are also tired, but her hair is neat and her clothes fresh. Papa puts a hand on the boy's small shoulder.

"You startle the tea leaves when you pour water so hot. They become bitter."

The boy holds the pot with both hands. "Then what do I do?"

"Now you wait," she says, lifting her hand from him.

9

Mazzu stumbles through the home then climbs upstairs for more sleep. When he wakes again, his room is brilliant. The sun glares off his mirror and walls. He turns onto his stomach and tries to fall asleep again. He sits up and, pulling his shirt to his nose, breathes in a dark scent. As he inhales, memories flare through him.

He goes down the stairs, turns the corner into the kitchen, and stops. The mayor is on her hands and knees. She looks over her shoulder as she pushes a towel over the floor.

"I knocked over the milk. It was nearly full too."

"Why didn't you call for me?"

"You were sleeping."

"Just wake me. I can be cleaning this."

"I can do it too. When it was just me here, who do you think did the cleaning?" Papa crawls over the floor, reaching with the cloth, corralling the runaway pool. With her hair unfastened, her stomach hanging over her pants, and her sleeves pushed up her arms, the mayor's age pierces the boy. Brown spots speckle the mayor's arms and the back of her hands.

They're on her neck too. She breathes heavily as she crawls over the floor.

Mazzu takes the towel from the mayor. He wrings it into the sink. "You have other things to be worrying about." With his foot, the boy pushes the towel around the floor. The mayor uses the counter to help herself up. She steps back while the boy dries the floor. "Why are you standing there? I can finish this. Look at you. Look at your pants. You have to go change. Go to your office or go into town. Don't just leave things to Bhara."

With the floor rinsed and the broken glass wrapped up, the boy washes his hands and face and goes into the basement. Mazzu picks up the cards from the stairwell and collects the pile from between the bars.

"How come you're awake again?" Babello asks. "You just slept a couple of hours."

"When I wake up and the room is bright, then I'm just awake. There's nothing I can do."

The bones of Babello's chin and cheeks stand through his beard. Sometimes, with the heat, Babello pushes his sleeves up, baring his narrowed arms. Mazzu realizes he is between two people who are rotting: one upstairs, groping for solutions; the other here in the basement, refusing all he encounters.

"You look like a scarecrow, Bello. You've become a scarecrow. I should bring you a mirror so you can see."

"No. Don't do that."

Unsure how to address Babello's mourning, Mazzu lingers. "How are you, Bello?" the boy repeats, at a loss for what else to say.

Babello shakes his head. With his feet, he plays with the fresh grass, brushing his soles over the blades. Wind gusts through the window, and they can smell the smoke that carries across town from the burning Plum Building. Mazzu sits with Babello through an afternoon's silence.

§

Upstairs, in his office, Bhara considers a list of methods to counter violence and crime, and to bolster public safety. He is pleased with the creativity of his advisors and the range of options with which they supplied him. When Bhara hears the sleepy boy shuffling around upstairs, he leans his head back, calls for the boy and waves him into his office.

"Would you like to sit? I thought we could talk. I realize this must be hard for you," Bhara says. "This fire. Given how your own parents"—Bhara searches for the appropriate word—"perished. Are you having nightmares? The mayor and I talked. We understand that the circumstances—that fire, and this day-to-day situation—are hard on you. That there's something cruel in locking up an arsonist in the space where you work. I understand you're doing a duty for the town." A feeling of generosity springs up through Bhara like a wild plant. "I have a spare room. If you'd like to live in my home, with me and my wife, while Babello is here, both of us would welcome you."

The boy shakes his head, retreats to his bedroom, and takes off his shirt.

"We have a nice home," Bhara calls from his office. Bhara talks through the boy's closed door. "It's calm and quiet. We could put a bed in my office for you. We cook nicely and simply, and we have a garden."

Bhara returns to his office, warmed by his own spirit. *I'll revisit this*, he decides, *in a day or two, when he's more open to suggestions.* Taking up a piece of paper and debating for a moment whether he truly completed the task, with a single stroke of his pen he crosses *Comfort boy* off his list of duties.

§

The Plum Building fire rages, leaping up and collapsing through a nearby wall, then spreading, scattering families who live nearby. People watch from hills and bridges. The fire shifts within the building and walks over floors and curls from roof to roof. Two who try to escape through it die days later from burns. The protests persist in some parts of the town, the dancers' shadows thrown back behind them. And with it, the drumming, stamping, and the songs of awakening persist.

Following the second fire, a gutted factory that has been abandoned comes under cooperative rule. On the weekends, overturned crates are arranged into a stage for a burgeoning style of theatre. The melancholy plots and rhetoric comfort those who watch. Why have only the elite been empowered? one woman asks, raising a hand in the makeshift theatre. The audience nods at the insufficiency of patience as a way to gain prosperity. In another play, agreeing to a role called "sky," Isabella descends from the scaffold, climbs out of a harness, and after fifteen minutes of witnessing a simulation of the city's workings, she turns, an alien among the day-to-day anxieties of the actors. What I am seeing, she says, is utter inhumanity.

She weights the phrase so adeptly it has the added resonance of personal sincerity. In other plays, the action halts at the climax and the audience pieces together the fairest ending. With their imaginations stirred, they turn their interrogations to the town itself.

Zuraffi's plays, once considered dazzling, are chastised. They are torn open and ravaged, cul-de-sacs of richly abstruse plot analyzed for their political shortcomings. In real life, one playwright says, there aren't miracles. If we wait for miracles to bring justice, we'll be waiting forever. We must bring justice.

If these townspeople crave a defensive outcry from Zuraffi, they have failed. In lieu of any counterstrike, she maintains her committed silence. Why does she say nothing? they wonder. After all we've given, why does she say nothing when she's most needed?

The price of coffee and of bread rises, as do trespassing, house-sharing, and theft. The irritated merchants clamour for stronger punishments to deter the reaching hands, and more and more people cluster at the theatres, where they pray, chant, and pass out pieces of fruit or bread at the end of the night's invigoration. On one inside wall of the factory, a yellow-tinted mural of Babello's younger brother appears, his head tilted to receive an aura of light.

§

During those days of violence, people hurry in and out of the mayor's home, bringing graphs, opinions, and arguments.

In the basement, the boy turns on his padded stool. Before he met Babello, Mazzu's main influences were the mayor,

Zuraffi's poems, and the trove of books on the library shelves. But now, thanks to his conversations with Babello, there is an undercurrent to Mazzu's understanding. Sometimes Mazzu listens with skepticism and other times with undisguised rejection, so the prisoner's logic attaches to deeper portions of the boy's brain, nagging at him, priming him for another stage in life.

"Should we play to ten thousand, Bello? Should we just add to our score day after day until the winner is the first one with thousands or millions?"

With the bars and leaves between them, the boy sits across from the dissident, walking into Babello's past. Babello doesn't waste energy by answering abstractly; he draws on episodes from his life. The boy drives on, posing question after question.

"You think Papa is unjust? Bello? You think she is unjust?"

"Can someone who can't understand be unjust? The town can't be fixed by pleasing people one at a time, or appealing to someone's goodwill. We've outgrown her."

§

"Bello!" the boy chirps, coming into the basement, trying to lift the prisoner's mood. "Throw away the records. Throw away all those accounts that give perspective. Today, Bello, it is truly hot. It is so hot today that even the most industrious of us are napping! Children are counselling parents out of tears. Bello, even the lovers have lost their zeal!"

Babello bites his lip. He is in tears, with his back turned, unable to shake off the smell of smoke. "Mazzu—"

It has been three days since Issan lit the Plum Building on fire and died inside it. Impatient for the prisoner to shed his mourning, Mazzu continues, "The fiercest debaters, Bello, are admitting the severity of this heat without quarrel…"

§

Following instructions from the mayor, two noisy guards come down the stairs and unlock the gate of the basement cell. The boy swivels on his stool. The guards grip the gate and, timing their effort, jerk it aside. The metal screeches and the vines strain. Their roots tug soil up.

"Stand," one guard barks. "Stand. Come, stand up."

"Stand," the other guard orders with a more menacing tone.

They step over the trough. They crack Babello on the back and pull him by the shoulders. Babello holds the bars and struggles with the guards. When they hit him again, Babello screams. One of the guards pries at Babello's bony fingers, while the other pulls the prisoner by his stomach. They peel his fingers off the bars. They hit him a third time. The guards lift him from the floor and prop him up and search Babello's hair with their thumbs. They push his chin up high and search his beard.

"There's no blue sky and green grass to see where you're going."

"Will you miss your garden? Where you're going there's only stone underfoot. Hey? You have nothing to say?"

"This one doesn't talk?" the first guard asks.

"No," Mazzu says.

The guards push Babello up the stairs and into the sunlight.

The cell gate remains ajar. The boy walks into that space and lifts his arms. He imagines spending eighteen days there. He takes off his shoes and walks over the grass. Mazzu looks through the bars at his workbench, his stool, and then at the stairwell, imagining the perspective Babello had during their talks. He walks over the stones and understands why Babello walked the way he did, transferring his weight between his feet so judiciously. Despite the grass, the pieces of stone sting. Returning to the mattress, Mazzu sits in the posture Babello assumed in the morning. He looks at the opposite wall, then at the meagre provision of sky. He imagines sixteen days with just water in his stomach. Sitting in that cell, the boy decides to skip his dinner; then, judging this measure too skimpy, he promises himself he will fast until the following night.

Upstairs, Mazzu finds the mayor and asks about the two guards who took Babello. Overhearing this, Bhara bounds around the corner and joins them.

"No, I don't want him here. I don't want him in this house any longer," the mayor says. "He shouldn't have been here at all. You were right. It is your space. It was a mistake of us to use that cell."

"But it's fine, Papa. He was fine here."

"And the problem with the rats is solved now too," Bhara says. "No prisoner, no rats." He smiles. He puts a hand on the boy's shoulder.

"Do you want to have tea?" the mayor asks.

The boy nods.

Bhara follows behind them. They are in the midst of a kitchen discussion when they hear cries from outside.

The front door swings open and bangs against the wall. The two guards push Babello back across the carpet and down the hallway.

"Prison riot," one guard yells ahead to the mayor. They push Babello, who bucks and resists them. His lips and nose are bleeding. His forehead is red and swollen with a welt. Babello upsets one of the hall tables. A rope binds his sweating wrists. Another rope cinches his ankles, runs up his back, and wraps his neck. The guards try to herd him, but he lunges, knocking them side to side, slamming against them. Babello trips over one of their feet, straining the rope. In the confusion, the guards' hats fall. When one of the guards bends to pick them up, Babello knees his head into the wall. The guards jab at his sides, but they restrain themselves from retaliating with full force in front of the mayor's calm dignity. One of them grabs Babello by his neck.

"What happened?" Bhara asks. "What is this?"

"I spoke the truth! I went in and yelled out the truth of this town and they all understood!" Babello resists both guards at the stairwell, stubbornly refusing to duck down. "Bhara, I read your treatises a year ago. I read them, Bhara." He stamps to get his attention. "I'm talking to you." The guards strike him. Babello pushes back with a shoulder, knocking one guard against the wall. Babello uses the other shoulder to wipe his cut lip, then sucks on it. "I'm talking to you. You wanted to talk to me before, now I want to talk to you. Do you see your mistakes now? Have you seen the gap between system and life?" Babello stands in the hallway with his damp chest heaving.

With his arms crossed, Bhara is primed and ready to assist the guards. "It's the peril of being an autodidact," Babello says. "Our laws are as innocent as you."

The guards push him downstairs and across the basement. Babello trips, a foot catches against the trough and he falls on his chest and chin. The guards kick his feet into the cell. The gate slams, the key pivoting in the lock. Babello squirms on the ground.

On their way out of the mayor's house, the guards brief Bhara and the mayor. "It wasn't him."

"It was already seething in the prison," says the other guard. "They all heard about the second fire. The prisoners were agitated, and Babello came in and they went mad."

"It was berserk," the first guard says, shaking his head. "But none of us were really hurt."

"What did he yell?" Bhara asks.

"It began even before he started yelling. I don't think they could hear anything he said."

"They saw him—"

"They knew him."

"—and he was jumping around, and they loved it and went wild."

The guards wait for the mayor, then realize that she has no directive to offer, so they leave and cross the town with their heads down. They take the long route along the river before returning to the general jail.

§

When Mazzu returns into the basement, he sees Babello sitting on the floor. Reaching through the gate, Mazzu knifes the bloodstained rope off his ankles and wrists. Babello unknots the rope from his neck and gently holds his neck with both hands.

Mazzu pulls the rope to his side of the basement, coils it up, and hangs it from a hook. "Bhara won't ever forgive you. You'll be here forever now. He'll let you die here. I don't even know how many years he'll keep you locked up." The boy takes an apple from the tray and sets it on Babello's side. "Now you just have to eat. There's no choice. It's been forced on you." As he sits, he notices that his own hands are bloody.

"Could you get me a needle and thread?"

"What for?"

Babello shows his torn shirt.

"Are you hearing me? You'll be here forever! You'll never be free. You humiliated Bhara in front of others. Do you know what that means? Do you know what humiliation does to him? That isn't even your shirt, Bello! Who cares if it's torn. You shouldn't have lost your temper. He'll leave you here without any qualms. He's absolute. He's not…he's not like anyone you've met. This is your coffin now, Bello. Do you understand? You just have to eat now." The boy tosses the hardened breadroll at Babello, who catches it and sets it down on the ledge.

Babello waits until after the boy has gone, then flings the food from the window. He watches birds squabble over it.

§

With the riots, and the tide of public opinion still susceptible to influence, Bhara and the mayor huddle with a group of merchants and advisors in the mayor's disordered office and debate what to do about the rumours, the newspaper stories, the town's hot mood, and finally what to do with the arsonist in the basement. "Well, there is still the general prison," Bhara says. "Today may well have been a fluke. We could try again. If we send Babello back a second time, the superintendent will want to prove himself. He won't let that happen twice."

"Anything else?" the mayor asks.

"Anything else? What do you mean?"

"What else is there? What other options are there?"

"You mean, let him free?" Bhara says with astonishment. "But…you mean as a goodwill gesture? To placate people? I don't think—"

The mayor nods. "Yes. That's choice two. And? Is there a third choice?"

They all look at each other.

"Execution?" Bhara says.

"I don't want him staying with Mazzu any longer," says Papa. "He confessed. He has no remorse. He doesn't acknowledge the town's laws."

"We can't execute someone who's fasting."

"He has too much support in the town."

"People will be outraged. You'll be finished. We'll be shamed too. We won't live it down."

"One week is what I give," says Papa. "One week is what he can spend here, then he's gone. Bhara, this is your responsibility. You wanted him jailed separately. You have four options. Solve this."

§

Meanwhile, through the town, in the closed and open markets, Baraffo's riots multiply. They rove from street to street. With the mayor's backing, Bhara implements a town-wide curfew, which is ignored. People gather and chant into the night.

In the mayor's busy hilltop house, with influential citizens hurrying up and down the stairs, the boy listens until he hears the silence that informs him he's finally alone. Mazzu opens a cupboard. He climbs onto a chair and, stretching for a shelf, takes down a jar with two hands. He unscrews the lid and spoons salt into a glass that he then fills with warmed water. He swirls the water, tastes it, and grimaces. He pours out half of it, adds more water, and checks the subtler, diluted taste. On other occasions in the next few days, the boy will administer a similar portion of sugar. In the basement, Mazzu passes these glasses between the vines to Babello, who drinks back the water. When Babello does question the taste, the boy simply shrugs. "Well water," he says. "It always changes. It's not like rainwater."

At night, in the otherwise empty house, a lamp burns in the basement. After several tries, Babello coaxes the thread into the needle. His shirt buckles around the seam he sews. He stitches the tear the two guards made, then snaps the thread in his teeth and pulls the shirt back over himself, hiding his torso.

The boy notices a change. After Babello's forced march across town toward the general prison, during which he was cheered by the townspeople, and the altercation with the guards and the chief aide, Babello is alert, and his mind and tongue decisive again.

"I've been thinking," Babello says. "I don't think they're right about Issan. He wouldn't die like that. He wouldn't have killed himself. Issan wouldn't do that. It must have been someone else. They have it wrong. And if Issan thinks they suspect him he would flee. He wouldn't talk on his own behalf and reason it out. So, he's likely off hiding somewhere."

"It was him, Bello."

"People don't just change like that. It wasn't him. He wouldn't do that. I'm telling you."

"It was him, Bello. No one's disputing that. His face is up on walls around town. Everyone agrees. They're chanting his name."

"When you see the mayor alone, ask her. Maybe she doesn't want to say it in front of others. Maybe she's hiding something. Or find Isabella and ask her. He wouldn't lie down and let himself burn. That isn't who he is. That's not his nature."

"Bello...no one's questioning it. No one. People are calling him a hero. They think he's brave. They think he did what was right. They're grateful. They've memorized his face. They revere him. It was him, Bello. I'm sorry."

"I promise you. He wouldn't do this."

The boy waits a moment. "Then you misread him."

Babello looks between the leaves at the boy. "But how could I have misread him by so much?"

PART 3

10

Following Baraffo's second fire and the elegies and tributes to Issan, and with Babello growing thin in the hilltop jail, Isabella found herself tiring quickly. Assuming it was grief, she went to sleep early and spread her arms out over the bed's width. As her complexion brightened, and the rumours of the change sped through the town, she sent out confidantes with her own explanations. She spoke with former teachers, classmates, and friends who listened courteously, but afterward they reported the changing hue of her skin and made insinuations. Isabella sighed and shook her head. She consulted her older sister, Sara, who measured the colour of her arm against Isabella's. "That difference is only because of the sun," Sara muttered. She pushed her sleeve up, and the two sisters pressed their shoulders against each other. Sara looked at Isabella with concern but then hugged her. "You're fine," Sara said, with her conquering smile. "You're just perfectly fine."

Isabella willed her cherry-coloured body through the final days of the grieving ceremonies for Issan. Through those days of lethargy, Isabella's face and demeanour simulated the empathy she lacked the capacity to feel. It was as if she had consumed an anchor that lay across her hips. She dragged herself around until her back buckled and she lay in bed moaning, kicking off the stifling sheets, then crawling across the mattress to pull them back over her, while refusing friends who brought soup.

Isabella stayed in bed.

In those days, the people of Baraffo who heard of her changing skin and thickening sputum buttoned up their undyed clothes of mourning and converged on that room. Classmates, relatives, those to whom Isabella owed money, men who had been proudly in love with her, others who hid their adoration behind erratic friendships, women friends, and townspeople who simply went to see her out of propriety, visited with their bowls of medicinal soup. The bowls covered the floor of her room and flavoured the air. Two friends who arrived together mistook them for an array of chamber pots charting the trends of her body's wayward filtration.

Isabella churned in bed, sweating through successive sheets. Her hair was a dark clump that Sara spread over the pillow so it could air out. Isabella's eyes became bloodshot, and she emitted an odour that her sister ignored. The people of the town consoled her without believing the soothing words they spoke.

Assuming her death was imminent and fearing that they would be outed as outside the circle of her intimates, some friends pre-empted her passing and inundated Isabella's room with flowers—marigolds, tulips, wooden buckets of lilies—and cards with messages of consolation. They competed to be the town's most memorable eulogist. Those attending to her gathered vases, glasses of water, and bowls for the excessive flowers, cut the stems, and selected appropriate perches. But when the supply of vessels was exhausted, the bunches were leaned along the walls, then simply held for a moment before they were dropped on the floor and kicked away. Some people of Baraffo, afflicted with envy, gossiped that her evasion of death indicated a vanity or showy performance and that she was overly fond of extracting gifts. "It's a tactic," they warned, raising a finger. "She is pilfering from us—even while our town suffers."

With the Plum Building still smouldering, Isabella's health became the touchstone of Baraffo's thoughts. The fire was too vast and dire to stand beside, so a portion of the town elected to stand over her sickbed instead.

That floral smell tided in her bedroom air. It shifted with the wind as though it were a single, sail-like petal. The petals that had loosened from their stems and fluttered free matted the floor and cascaded down the stairs and blew from her doorway out into Baraffo's streets. Those flowers that arrived with her second wave of presumed death were accepted with grace then thrown promptly out of the window.

When Isabella tired of hearing overwrought letters of consolation seasoned with uplifting reminders that death was inevitable, a thin man with a resonant voice was hired and stationed on the street near her window. Throughout the daylight hours, and twice in the night, he leaned a ladder into a tree to find a high branch to stand on and broadcast his cry: "Not dead!"

"Not dead! Not dead!" His cry pierced the activities of Baraffo's merchants, the craftsmen, postmen, officials, coffee sellers, inmates, poets, students, the indolent, the desperate, and the radicals. At the approach of each hour, conversations and activities quieted and the people of Baraffo hushed each other, waving their arms for silence, and inclined their heads toward their window and stood at a standstill—"Not dead!"— before smiling and carrying on what they were doing with freshened enthusiasm.

The town crier took it on himself to expand his duties and police the conversations surrounding Isabella and Sara's home. If he overheard any hint of elegy, he interrupted these talks with a simple but firm swing of his arm. "The time is not near."

On the eighth day of Isabella's illness, by which time the crier was hoarse and his shouts lacked their earlier glory, and while Isabella lay in bed swollen and layered in sweat, the spoonfuls of coloured powders arrived. Fed by the rumour that Isabella had resisted death, aged half-blind women stood on stools and, reaching for their high kitchen shelves, twisted open jar after jar, identifying each powder by smell. With their little fingers, they stirred the chosen powders into serving spoons of honey and walked across town bearing these spoons with the stature that the certainty of their cure endowed. They bumped into Isabella's room and forced their spoons through the gates of her mouth. The spoons piled up on the other side of her bed; each new spoon that she pulled from her lips was released by her left hand and clinked down the pile, rolling and turning end over end, until it caught.

Isabella was heaped in quinine, mobbed in aloe, and poisons were sprinkled on her too in the hope that these would repulse the pathogens she housed.

In her delirium and estrangement from Baraffo's attitude and thought, what Isabella failed to understand was that her foul-smelling body was, first through accelerating cycles of gossip, then the indisputable gusto of the town's newspaper columns, understood to be the concentrated site of the town's suffering. In emotional appeals, the merits of the iconography were detailed. So, through a mixture of communal exhortation, goodwill, superstition, and what they knew of medicine, chanting, and prayer, the people of Baraffo rallied behind her with the conviction that by saving her, they could, in turn, save what they loved.

Those who were old enough, in the rickety generation one link above the blind, could not help noticing in this symbolism a satisfying match with the town's abandoned ritual of sacrifice—years ago, before the summer harvest, on the day of the longest sun, one child would be thrown several feet up into the air to sate the whimsical beast who lorded over Baraffo. After three or four throws, if their lord did not kneel to snatch up the child, they felt obliged, due to a general hatred of half measures, to kill it themselves. What was happening with Isabella seemed to be the opposite. "We want her to live," repeated these arthritic townspeople, scoring the logic of it into their tough, experienced brains, "so that *we* can live." They raised their arms with the significance of it. Those who dimly understood this revelation, but, out of humility or modesty, were unwilling to espouse it as their elders had, subdued themselves and nodded.

But the gifts, flowers, solemn notes, and conflicting powders delivered to Isabella were unable to rejuvenate her.

"Not dead," the crier croaked from his familiar branch. "Not dead," he called wearily, beginning to find fault with his vocation. "Not dead," he sighed, holding a low branch and only halfway climbing his ladder.

She lay on her back. Her tongue was black, and speckles encrusted the surface.

At the end of the first week of her illness, Isabella's legs retreated from their scarlet phase and tightened. Her skin darkened, became grey, and her flesh lost that elasticity, that pleasing give to the touch. Poised on that bed, with the fingers of one hand against her brow and her other hand open, she became a stone.

A tribunal assembled on one side of her bedroom. They invoked Babello. "Her beloved has gone," said one who valued proximity. "And not knowing when he would return, she is giving into death."

"No, it is that he betrayed her," ventured another. "One must dedicate one's life to a single love. One mustn't disperse one's heart as he has across different interests." They created three plans to overcome Babello's incarceration, but Sara stamped these out as risky.

When Isabella's sister had her back turned, the people of Baraffo groped Isabella with impunity, sweeping their hands over her. They squeezed her calves and arms. Others tried biting her.

"She's eternal," a stricken man whispered, shy though he was of deities. Another interpreter of her illness disagreed. "We become our worst fault. She was an actor. She lacked true compassion." People tapped on her arms and tried crumbling pieces from her hair and toes. "Yes, it is because she did not truly feel," the literalists murmured. "She's becoming an oyster," a girl with braided hair sang while holding Isabella's foot. The tribunal laughed and repeated the judgment and patted the light-haired girl. Her mother knelt beside the child and whispered, "Why?"

"An oyster, an oyster, an oyster!" she sang, and threw a helping of petals into the air and danced, crudely lifting each knee into the air without rhythm, while the petals fluttered down on her.

Even when Isabella's pulse vanished, escaping the trace of the inquiring fingers, no one uttered the word *cadaver*. With their need for a healthy future, the people of Baraffo opted instead to call her "the convalescent."

Sara coaxed three boys to stalk the basement window of the mayor's home and throw balled-up pages in to Babello. They climbed the wooded hill and crawled toward the prison window, but guards spotted them and frightened them. These stammering students vowed to never again contravene a town-issued order.

§

"Not dead!" he cried. "Not dead! Not dead!" His voice boomed around the vicinity of the small home.

Children tested Isabella. They whispered confessions to her and tried shooting breaths to tickle her, but she wouldn't startle. Another child whistled into her ear, the warm air becoming shrill as it passed through gapped teeth. Then a superstition arose. The people of Baraffo, sure that their untutored children were attuned to natural insights, observed their offspring's fascination with Isabella's ears and began leaning over her to utter their desires and wishes. Some asked for peace, esoteric knowledge, mercy from physical pain, some asked for progeny, health, and others who leaned over her wanted what was already close at hand.

A sculptor on the brink of tears stood over her, wearing boots and grey clothes. Feeling himself charged again, he left her bed and paced the cliff beside the mayor's home. After witnessing her, he wanted to give up the efforts of his forty-six years of work, but because of the seeds of monstrosity that littered him and flourished in his concentrated art, he pushed his way back into her bedroom and felt the stone waves of her hair, the elbows, the ankles, the stalled throb in her veins, the lashes of her open eyes…"Yes," he murmured, with beastliness surging in him. Sara pulled his hands off her—he was stroking Isabella's cheek again and again—but he defied Sara, leaned forward, and kissed Isabella's lips, as if she were not stone but one capable of reply. He confessed his adoration for her and laid his head on her stomach before Sara pulled him off Isabella, flung him down their stairs, and, armed again with an ideal, he immersed himself in the harrows of his sole and devotional work.

As the gatekeeper to her sister's room, and because of her own grief, Sara struggled to discern the mourners from those who came to speculate and join in the room's chatty community. That bedroom became a gathering place filled with cut flowers. Visitors shared snacks and stories, savoured the atmosphere, played cards. The aged people of Baraffo who could not stand for the full length of these festive days asked that a bench or two be carried up the stairs for their sake.

Putting up a curtain, Sara separated the pointless joy and pain of the card players from the coterie of more sympathetic friends. As they dealt hands and kept score, the card players glanced at the curtain and guessed what transpired behind it based on the tones they overheard. After a few hours, agitated by this guesswork, they hassled Sara until she tore the curtain down and they saw that Isabella was not so different as their imaginations lured them to believe.

Sara frowned through the complaints of the indignant men who lectured her about the impropriety of the card players being so close by the ailing body. "We have been here longer than you," one card player shouted back, and with a sweep of his arm he cast the egotists away; offended, they roamed the town, recounting their rejection to everyone they met.

At night, Sara herded people from the bedroom. "I have the cure," one man said as he was being guided out. "But I would like something in return," he said, pulling Sara by the waist.

Five friends rocked Isabella side to side while Sara snapped off the bedsheet and spread a fresh one. She used a cloth to wipe the day's accretions from her sister. She wet the cloth again and pushed it over Isabella's legs and hair and hands. She wiped Isabella's eyelids, her toes, and beneath her knees. Each night, Sara washed the stone.

Sara ate alone, with a plate on her lap, and slept beside her sister. She woke at sunrise when the visitors knocked on the door downstairs. Half-asleep and clumsy, she accepted their hugs.

With Bhara ignoring Sara's pleas and forbidding her to visit Babello, Sara stood near her sister without knowing what to do. Did Babello know about her sickness? she wondered. Would the mayor tell him? Or the boy who lived with the mayor—would he tell?

At the outset of the second week, overcome with distress, Sara loosened the supply of her family's assets and put a reverse bounty on her sister's body, funnelling all of the town's knowledge and good intentions toward Isabella in exchange for the jewellery that tumbled through the generations of her family, as well as the chairs, tables, and other useful things that could be found in their home. People arrived asking her to confirm the offer. After litigiously parsed back-and-forths, Sara threw her arms into the air and offered the house too. News of this prize spread through the farmlands and up into the mountains and over them. The solitaries who resided in a network of caves heard it with pessimism. They made treks to confer with others who lived in green creases buffered by the mountain's winds to confirm the veracity of these rumours.

In town, theorizing that high emotion could inspire Isabella from her sleep, a group of musicians climbed her stairs. They rearranged the benches and played a first set with delicacy. Their melodies emerged like ribbons from their clipped fingernails. They soothed the other listeners, but Isabella was unmoved.

Then a radiant-faced flute player wearing tight clothes arrived. But the jauntiness of his playing and marching and the slight dance he did with his shoulders did not awaken her flesh; rather, Isabella's thorough sleep drained the sprightliness from his lips and he kept having to tug his tunes from the gravity of a dirge. The people gathered in that bedroom were transfixed by what he had just invented. They called for their friends to come and urged him to continue. He played on, despite the hollowness in his core and the pain in his lips and arms, his music wandering between his jaunty, merry aspect—when his elbows flapped at his sides—and the requiem, when he would stand still and pipe out a new strain of melancholy that troubled him.

Once the flute player begged his way out of the bedroom, a theatrical troupe arrived with a trunk of props. The actors held up a dark curtain and changed behind it. The elders of Baraffo sitting on the benches rejoiced at the farces, smiled at the pleasing contrivances of the tragedies, and experienced unbearable sorrow during the summery comedies.

Once the troupe, like the musicians and the flute player, had failed to rouse Isabella from her stony convalescence, lovers in the midst of courtships and burning with their fires pestered Sara until she allowed them to be fulfilled near the resting body. Baraffo's newest couples covered the bedroom floor. When their method failed as all the others had, the musicians, who had been standing outside squabbling, argued their way back into the bedroom. This time they played without order, shaking Isabella with the violence of disturbed art. Attracted by this discord, the lovers returned, lay down again on the petal-matted floor that thrilled with the vibrations of the music, shed their clothes, and in their mania they were no longer sure whose shoulder was whose, nor, with the icon so close, did they care. Even over the music, their cries could be heard across town, embarrassing some citizens.

Sara ordered that the room be cleaned. The benches and floor and bed frame and walls were washed, and the rug was thoroughly shaken and hung from the balcony. Despite the heat, Sara burned candles to treat the air. At night, as she was about to sleep, Sara sang a piece of a song. She touched Isabella's grey forehead.

With the news of Sara's offered bounty spreading across the region, nomadic creatures dressed in mismatched pelts arrived in Baraffo. These hermits wandered through the town, climbed the stairs, and found the room where the sick one lay. Hardly conversant, they frightened Sara, who pleaded for her classmates to force them to leave. These sunburned creatures ate while they spoke and let their exposed arms, chests, and legs boast of their strength. They were so large they were banned from sitting on the benches. One of these nomads stood over Isabella and, with his hefty arms, he raised a cudgel over her head. As he was about to smash her, he was pulled down by three of Babello's friends. They subdued his thrashing body. One friend dragged the wailing nomad by the shoulders and forced him down the stairs.

A new wave of authorities arrived. Sara stood aside while they plied Isabella's softening flesh with what knowledge and medical equipment they had. The town's healers bored holes into her and tugged sluggish blood from her ankles, swirling the blood that they had collected in glass bowls that they held up to the sunlight with both their hands. Patting her, they searched her flesh for tumours. They flayed her with branches until Sara's crying upset them, then stood aside while the leaves were collected into a pile and brushed down the stairwell. They bound Isabella's head with a rope and tightened the slack until Sara jumped up and screamed. Sara pulled the rope from Isabella's mouth and nose. A man who held an awl with wavering confidence was held back from tunnelling through the layers of her brain.

The people of Baraffo remained there, hour after hour, unable to pry themselves from her. With the benches moved away, Isabella's bed was pushed against the window and the diaphanous drapes were torn down so she lay in the after-noon's full, rehabilitative light.

After two days, when she was able to twitch again, a soft-spoken man lay on the floor and, with Isabella propped up over him, he pushed his thumbs into her feet. This man, who had spent months preoccupied by experiments on animals in the conduction of pain, pinched her skin along each bone while watching her face for any tingle of pleasure. When that day's healers trudged off to sleep, he turned her over and walked slowly up and down her as though her spine were a tightrope.

After a week of their efforts, the medics relented, shook their heads and backed away.

Then long-haired mystics arrived, descending on the town from the whirling air of the mountains. They came up the stairs into her room with their proud hats and inundated her with fruit pastes and forced her to drink glasses of tea that had been steeped in torn up leaves.

Initially ignoring her, this group of esoteric men, who the people of Baraffo knew of only by tall tales and chatty rumours, arrived and stood with their backs to her and extracted from Isabella's caregivers the details of her diet and virtue. Did she eat flesh, they asked, when Sara, due either to evasiveness or innocence, failed to discern the question's intent. The mystics gave formal nighttime addresses to the onlookers that detailed the day's progress, the pitfalls the night would bear, and the following day's correction. An evening balm was layered onto the skin of her arms, legs, and, after she turned over, her neck and back. They pushed the paste through the complexities of her feet. Holding her arms back as though they were the wings of a crane, they knelt on the bed, daubing her armpits with a cloth, then studied her modest tinkle of urine.

The mayor passed daily into her room, often with the boy at her side, stared at Isabella, and read the expressions of the well-wishers. The boy squirmed through the crowd, walked up to Isabella and touched her ankles. Papa pulled Mazzu back to her side, gave good wishes to all there, and left.

Hoping a visit from Babello would be the cure, Sara left to try her persuasions on Bhara, who stopped her with the sureness of his large hand. Others tried too, but with the mayor unwilling to hear any more about Babello, the chief aide bullied these petitioners into silence.

Isabella woke enough to murmur in her room. "You're not dying," one friend whispered, lifting Isabella's head onto her knee. Her friend took the cloth from her forehead, freshened it, and spread it out again. Isabella faded in and out of conversation. She talked through her confusion and stirred in bed.

Locking their fingers together into a seat, two friends carried Isabella into the bathroom and lowered her into the tub that they had half-filled. They washed her, then loosened the plug under her so the water swirled away. She was hugged with a towel then lifted to the bed, where she continued to murmur, her mind flipping erratically while she dropped from them back into hours of lifeless sleep. Her friends stood in the dark and followed the bedroom wall to the stairwell, mindful of that day's soup bowls, which sat on the floor for them like traps.

Isabella lay in bed, her plumper areas fuelling the hidden war her body fought against atoms that marauded and emptied her from within.

Her shins became visible. The network of bones interlaced across her chest protruded from her layer of skin. Her weight evaporated. Dampness hung in the room's enclosed air. Moss spread underneath her back, in the creases of her elbows and under her knees, and within the cloth-covered mattress. Isabella scratched at it, the moss coming off and clinging to her nails while petals blew in through the window, garnishing the old soup bowls.

At night, she bunched the bedsheets in her hands, uprooting them; as her mind flexed through hallucinatory dreams, she lay across the ridges of bedsheet in their wide gyre. When she woke into cognizance, she was morose. Lying in the dark, she cried until she sat up and coughs hurtled from her.

On the notepad that she had asked for to write letters to Babello, and with her mind degraded by illness, she scrawled inscrutable profundities until her hand weakened and she lost the pen. She slumped back into further hours of sleep and into dreams that perplexed her and challenged her belief that all things that happened in life were relevant, significant, and wholly ordained.

Needing fresh air, Isabella flipped the sheets off and staggered across the room on her weak legs. She tripped through the soup bowls, which overturned onto her feet, until she slipped sideways in the broth and lay there with her hair fanned out and her sleeping dress clinging to the floor, and kicked away the nearest bowls.

She sat in the bathtub, staring ahead while the water built around her hips, and then she leaned her hair back into the purifying stream. Visiting the next morning, friends paused when they saw the bits of potato, carrot, ginger, rice, and kidney beans littered over the tub and gathered into a hill that stopped up the drain.

They draped a shawl around her shoulders and helped her downstairs.

In those days of recovery and increasing energy, Isabella would turn and catch eyes averting from hers. Without any way to prevent it, Isabella became accustomed to being studied.

One day, she tried climbing the switchback stairwell up to the mayor's home, but her energy collapsed, and she sat on the leafy steps, recovering. Back home, she banished the experimental treatments that Sara had allowed—the remaining mystics and medics were castigated and sent forcefully away—and rested.

A dispute arose over who had been principally responsible for Isabella's recovery. Sara waved her hands and admonished everyone to wait for their due reward.

Isabella lay in bed with fluffed-up pillows under her, a glass on the window beside her, and a growing appetite. She bathed herself in the mornings and, to some encouraging applause, took walks, and the pigment of her skin reverted from grey, back through burgundy and a toxic orange, to its original hue.

The town's newspaper columnists shed their stateliness and jointly cheered her recovery. By the afternoon, their unison frayed once it was pointed out to them that they could not agree on the cause of her rejuvenation. In her skin and poise, each clique of writers read into Baraffo's own fortune. Some saw lessons, precedents, and moral imperatives; others, confident that the town's unseen spiritual enemy had been vanquished, leaped into the prophetic mode and scorned those abstractions that had been routed, and proclaimed Baraffo indomitable, eternal, her organs robust and her beauty no worse for wear.

With those proclamations of Isabella's recovery, the people of Baraffo squabbled over who should win the riches of Sara's promised prize. The newspapers weighed in, heating these arguments so that even those who felt their contribution had been modest (one of whom merely cited a calming influence that he naturally exuded) were inflamed and wanted what was rightly theirs. Even the cudgel-bearer, for whom neither paper advocated, and who could not claim one tangible benefit of his brief visit, had the temerity to return, scale a bookcase, and leave with Isabella's grandfather's misshapen guitar.

Sara divided the family belongings into two mountains of equal size and presented one to the mystics and the other to the medics. Each group dug through its pile and inventoried its bequest. One mystic pulled an eggbeater from the pile and toyed with it, turning the handle with a finger.

Each group looked at the other's pile and announced it was insufficient. Each demanded the house itself. The sisters chafed at this request for a couple of hours, then finally gave up their grandfather's house, the mystics agreeing to the second floor and the medics contenting themselves with the humbler ground floor.

Holding hands, the two sisters discussed what they should do as their possessions flowed from them. While they had these discussions, their home was stripped. The kitchen was picked clean, books were taken, and seldom-used relics were swiped from a beam. The potted plants were whisked away, and geraniums planted in front of the house were gently uprooted. The checkered rug Sara left hanging from the balcony rail was taken, as were the benches that the elders had sat on.

The people of Baraffo claimed their sworn compensation.

When the sisters woke one morning, they found that the curtain had been plucked from the window, the few rings had been slipped off of Sara's drowsing hands, and a chain had been separated and drawn from her neck. In the dark, her hand went to her neck to brush away what she assumed was a housefly. Sara's colourful repertoire of clothes were taken too, as were Isabella's earthy tones. And while she bathed one night, Isabella returned to the bed to find that the sheets and pillowcase had been stripped. She checked the balcony to see if her sister had rinsed them, but she didn't find them drying there. The pillow remained, as did the bed of her monumental sickness. She climbed onto it and, using the towel as a blanket, crumpled into nude sleep. When she woke and felt her face, she realized she no longer had her earrings.

When it became common knowledge that the two sisters did not know what to do to quell the week-long dispersal, an aged and obstinate woman arrived and counselled them. This elder remembered the traditions governing recoveries and won their attention with tales of other such material diasporas. She found a cloth for Isabella, showed her how to hold it to create a sack, and pushed the young woman out through the front door.

Dressed in the snug fabric, Isabella shuffled door to door through Baraffo as an alms seeker.

Not wanting to be presumptuous or signal the size of the gifts she needed, Isabella gathered the cloth in her hands until the basin of it was a fraction of its full size. Isabella supplicated, holding her hands out, so the townspeople could drop in any donated item. Dressed plainly and with her head covered so that the people of the town could not even know if it was her or her sister substituting for her, she received gifts. The established families of Baraffo milled in their homes waiting for her. After only a few homes, the cloth strained between her fingers with the weight of the homage. She returned to her bed and rested.

The people of the town bestowed squabbling birds, a blossom of magnolia, a vial of pine-scented perfume, a gleaming fish, and a child that swam in the sack until Isabella knelt and released him into daylight. They boasted of their gifts by pointing out what conspicuous thing their lives now lacked. Isabella shuffled around Baraffo. She received a fistful of coins, ceremonial dishes, promissory notes, fruits, bay leaves, a sheaf of paper, an oar, eighteen gentian seeds, a ladle, letters bearing proposals both playful and serious (she frowned as she read through the brash ones and their show of false force), there were other unsigned letters of more celestial praise, numerous instruments—and when they saw her struggling with the full bag, tugging it over the lawns and across ditches, the townspeople gave her a wheelbarrow that they loaded with clothes, wheat-coloured wine, an itinerant singer, tomatoes, sugar, a teapot, a recent nest, a drum, some knives, honey, a collection of odes to her knotted with an emerald thread, and, taped to one of the wheelbarrow's arms, a sheet of homilies that Sara and Isabella read in candlelight and pondered.

One man, lacking in appropriate tribute, and wanting to distinguish himself by giving her his greatest gift, swallowed a serum that serrated his vessels and horrified his flesh. This and other deaths were kept from Isabella: fanatics tore their page from the town's book with a dagger, a rope, a wooded gorge; someone experimented with a hunger strike. An anthologist bound an illicit collection of chronicles of these deaths, which wandered the spectrum from gallantry to absolute self-abasement. Contrary to the anthologist's intent, this book offered few insights into death and amounted instead to an expression of pathological devotion. With this dissident text in circulation and studied by the town's macabre eyes, Baraffo's first formal inquiries into beauty were born. Those women who resembled Isabella found themselves elevated in stature, and those men who resembled Babello gained in prominence too. Some women copied Isabella's style. They shed irony, sarcasm, and embellishments, and they no longer encumbered their hands or faces with ornaments; they tried to mimic her amiable, bright-faced directness.

Each morning, Sara and Isabella unpacked their gifts. Sara sat with a guitar on her lap, strumming it with a thumb, and watched as her sister's hands went again and again into the cloth sack.

One morning, the convalescent did not even venture out. She opened the door and found items laying before her—tasselled carpets, copper pots, a polymath, a shining golden horn, a conundrum, an oath for a term of labour, the contents of an orchard shaken into a wagon, a deed to a distant land, hairpins, sugarplum jam. There was the bust of an irrelevant ruler, an empty placard for her to craft whatever rebellious message she pleased, and a cistern filled with jewellery that the two sisters shared and tried on for one another, as if they were children again and toying with their identities.

The medics and mystics who wanted to begin their occupancy of the sisters' house endured the censure of the newspapers, which escalated from principled criticism to open wrath. The columnists assailed the usurpers' lack of humanity. The mystics and medics ignored these slanders and insisted that soon they would move in. Pragmatic above all else, the newspaper columnists swung their boats of tirade around and praised the usurpers for the fortitude to brave popular opinion and do what, frankly, was not so easy. The sisters were given a dreary house a widow had died in, leftover paints, and a sack of curtains. Sara and Isabella tore down the fabrics nailed over the hot windows, kept the door open to a cleansing wind, and scrubbed the floor.

Isabella was the first person who had no formal role in the town, but was known by all.

When she walked, people waved at her, but, wary of her stature, they restricted themselves to a reverential distance. Even those she knew well would not take her hand or step into an embrace. After the gropings and the layers of kisses when she was unconscious, she went entire days where the only human she touched was her sister. The rest of the townspeople crossed to the other side of the street when she approached, then turned to watch her shuffle by.

§

These were days when Isabella drank plenty of water, ate sparingly, and bruised easily.

The obstinate lady, who had revealed to the sisters the necessity of alms-seeking, led Isabella to an overgrown bathing area. Standing together beneath an uprooted tree that leaned over the pond, and with their ankles submerged, she lectured Isabella on the good health the site granted.

Isabella bathed in the fog of dawn, scooping cool water up her legs and stomach. Submerging and pushing off from the stone, she swam across the spring toward the far side, where wilted petals coated the surface. Insects skimmed by, creasing the water with their pin-like feet. Isabella disturbed this, spreading her arms and legs and turning onto her back. Leaves gathered against her coasting neck.

The children of the town snuck from their homes and followed her on those predawn walks to the spring, the girls absorbing her postures and gestures and her weakened gait, and the boys pawing at her. They touched her ankles, her arm—they pulled her hem and leaped for her loose-hanging sleeves. Though they were a nuisance, she decided their wonder was an innocent thing, and pulled herself away from their hands with courtesy, then used trees to brace her slide down the mud path to the pond.

Initially shy, the children crept closer and closer until they spied her during these habitual baths when she closed her eyes and, with her elbow raised, emptied the gourd over herself. Even once she heard them in the foliage, she couldn't reproach them. She crossed the dark water in slow strokes and returned to their side, where she held on to a rock with both arms and caught her breath.

Morning after morning, the pack of children followed her to her ritual bath. They leaned their elbows on a crumbled cobblestone wall and sat on loosened stones. They sewed the stems of lilies into wreaths they traded. They repeated whatever she said, and reused these expressions with their parents and teachers, so that those phrases embedded themselves in the town's changing sensibility. The flute player joined their procession, and while Isabella bathed, he piped a sunrise tune that raised his mood.

Skeptical of the sacredness this spot was purported to bear, Isabella nonetheless enjoyed her routine. Standing on that first stone, she lifted off her sleeping dress and left it hanging off a branch and sank into the water, whose temperature stunned her. Her hair fanned out, and she swam farther and farther each day. In her legs and core, she could feel herself approaching her old, lost power, that reservoir of unspoken resolution hidden by her demeanour.

Many of these children accompanied her during the day too, and walked as a squeaking shield ahead of her, insulating her from anything they judged as beneath her dignity and abusing anyone who treated her with vulgarity. They threw stones at those who leered and humiliated others whose jealousy was ludicrous.

Isabella climbed out of the water at dawn. She felt weak again and staggered on land as if her legs were made of stems. With the flute player piping a tune and flapping his elbows while she towelled behind a tree, Isabella tied her hair up and slipped into her day's dress. Using young trees, she pulled herself up the path and, with the children peeling off of her and scattering back to their homes, she crossed the town to her new house and sat inside with Sara and a pot of revivifying tea.

Her name became a totem to these children. They rarely uttered it, many outright refused, and referred to Isabella instead, as "she."

11

azzu extricates himself from Giulietta, lifting her hands from him. She gives in, letting him crawl out the window without much explanation. All he mumbles is, "I have to talk with someone."

"This late? Why? Hey, talk to me. Tell me."

There's a moment when he's about to turn back to Giulietta and empty himself to her and tell her about the mayor's decay, Bhara's lofty speeches within the mayor's home, the changes to Babello's face, and admit to the dread he feels—but instead he stays quiet and hurries off.

The boy crosses the smouldering town. He passes between a set of guards who stand halfway up the stairwell to the mayor's home. The boy coughs from the smoke. Inside the home, he steps downstairs, forgetting the lamp, so they have only the light the sky provides, which suffices.

Babello plays with the shoots of grass while he talks. He lays his hand on the floor, bending the grass, or he pinches a blade, drawing his fingers up its height. He isn't aware of these motions. Otherwise, Babello conserves his energy. He leans in the window, but he no longer paces the cell. With his hunger strike crossing the four-week threshold, Babello's body has entered its decisive phase of failure.

Just as hours earlier, when the boy's hands were on Giulietta and her mouth against his or at his ear, hurrying through her day's burst of thoughts and sensations, so now the boy is in the darkness with the thrill of Babello's memories, which also light up in Mazzu's imagination.

And just as the boy once paged through books, so now he sits, collecting a story the mayor wanted to repress. Babello's voice and focus vary. His conversation rarely ranges back before the previous year, so if the boy is asked, he can't quite fathom Babello existing as a child, mistake-prone and watchful, absorbed in games, or even Mazzu's own age, and lacking awareness and assurance. It seems to Mazzu that Babello walked in from the town's foothills as he is now, lean and tense.

Mazzu urges him ahead.

And just as the wind passes through the window and spreads through the cell, the man's perspective blows from his lips through the vine-wrapped bars of the gate into the caverns of the boy's mind. The boy pulls him away from stories of Issan, during which Babello fills the dark air with sighs and the talking is stalled by silences.

"Are they thinking of having me executed?" Babello asks, interrupting his own stream of thought.

"No."

"Can you tell me if you hear something?"

"They don't execute scarecrows, Bello. No one executes a scarecrow. It's never been done. Go on, Bello."

"People wanted some order, so we had two votes to see who would lead us. We were growing, people kept joining us, asking what they could do, adding more thought and spirit. We needed our dissent to have a strategy, to be organized. Without putting myself forward, I won the first vote. Out of about 320, I got 122. In the second vote, when people wanted a surer idea of who would be responsible, I was up to 225."

"You didn't put yourself forward?"

"No."

"What did Isabella do? Was she angry with you for this?"

"She thought I was working to win it. There was a week-long argument between us. I was trying to explain things, she took a cup of coffee from my hand and hurled it aside. She pulled books off a shelf—the books I loved and reread but that she didn't want in our home—and put them on the street for someone else to take. She said their arguments were changing me. She told me my nature was changing. She said I was being pulled away from her and deformed. She wanted me to meditate my anger away. She told me I was being seduced, that I was ceding my more natural self, and she asked me to remember who, at heart, I really was. She worried about what would happen if I was known as the leader. She knew Bhara. She sat in on lectures he gave, and she was fearful of his darkness. During those days, our only real days of not understanding each other, it felt like my world had capsized.

"After this second vote, one newspaper said Issan and I should both be banished. They told everyone that we hadn't recited the vows, and that we were a threat, and unworthy of Baraffo. They called us intruders and traitors, as if our family hadn't also come from this soil. So one night I stood on the fountain ledge and made a speech explaining this, and why I couldn't say those vows in good faith, and a newspaper printed it. Then we won even more supporters. So then the newspaper moved on from me and seized on Issan, saying he was a thief. They included an illustration of his face. But all he'd stolen was fruit or bread, or things people didn't even need. He believed food belongs to the person who is hungry. The newspaper said I was a criminal too since I looked after him. They pushed for us to both be banished from the town. They said that since we rejected the town's rules, the town had a right to reject us."

"Why wouldn't you just recite the *Sixteen Laws?*"

"What you don't understand is that Issan's life was never like yours. You were taken into the mayor's home. You've been given dinners and a place to sleep. You've been helped. Even when you can't see it, every day you're being helped. He was watched, suspected, checked on to see if he met all standards—and why? Because he was hungry?

"Isabella was fighting with him too. She didn't want him bringing stolen food home. She wanted him to stop this. She told him we could find a way to all share and be fine. Finding this quaint, Issan mocked her. Neither would give in. He would get offended by her and go off alone for four or five days, and then come back sullen and remote—even from me. She saw something in him. She worried about him. But I went through that phase too, so I didn't realize how bad his was."

The boy tilts his head. "Why is it quaint, Bello? Why is hating theft quaint?"

Babello disregards the question.

Mazzu weighs it all. "And now? Isabella still believes in you after the fire? She thinks that was a noble thing for you to do?"

"Yes."

"To go and burn down a building?"

"Yes."

"How could you do that with her against it? Why make your lives go different ways?"

"You don't believe me, but we'll be together soon. She hated that building. She thought the man who owned it was vile. She wrote an essay about him."

"But Bhara will never allow it. You'll never go free."

"Don't you feel it? This town is rising up. As long as I'm not executed, I'll see her soon."

"You don't think they would execute a hunger striker, do you. That's your wager?"

"How could they dare?"

"So they can't execute you, but he can let you die here. They will say it's your decision. Bhara will even see his own decision as principled. They won't let you go, Bello. You've taken it too far."

"If that happened, the mayor would be finished. Bhara would be finished. It would be their own deaths. And this house would be taken over by better people."

"What do you mean, 'finished'?"

"Imagine what will happen to this town. Imagine what will happen to all the people who believe in me. You think four guards will stop them from coming up the hill and into this home? There are thousands now."

"But Bello, I don't understand something. Why did people vote for you? Why you? You really weren't asking them? You weren't secretly going around and talking to them and convincing them you could lead? Why did they pick you?"

"We had meetings in our home. People were always coming over for tea or dinner or to ask Isabella for help with something. And then the meetings became so big that we were sitting on the floor and up the stairs, and then it was so many that we had to meet outside. They knew me."

"But things don't happen that way. People divide and squabble and want different things and different styles. How did they coalesce behind you?"

"I was probably the one known by most."

Mazzu mutters something and shakes his head.

12

One dawn, Isabella returns from her bath and finds her door open. She hugs herself with a blanket as the children who accompany her stream past her legs and call out in the darkness. They find a drawer of candles and rove with these lights, shining them on shelves and corners, then scurrying up the stairs.

Isabella watches the wands float through the home. The floors are bare. The shelves are emptied. As she enters the ransacked house, the horde of children go past her the other way to the street and startle the town with cries of larceny. With the town's parents astonished, disbelieving that the house of a feeble and beloved person could be robbed, these zealots search the streets of Baraffo, tumble through open windows, use stones to shatter closed ones, and rap on doors until the sleepers are awake. They search closets, tossing aside clothes, smash into trunks, peer beneath beds, and study lawns and gardens for any plots that look freshly dug.

From the shore to the encampment on the foothills, the infant redressers search Baraffo.

With the strengthening sun, the children drop their candles and continue their search with both hands. They paw at people's pockets, run away with keys, harangue everyone they meet, utter accusations, overturn the merchants' stalls, and search boats. They hunt through kitchens and sheds and surprise those who are still in bed by tearing off the sheets to see what they conceal. With their myriad little voices, they choir for Isabella's gifts to be returned.

Some parents stand aside and watch with pride at how injustice has inflamed their kin. "It is their moral compass," one father says. "We have raised them so well."

"It is from the heart," one aunt says, touching her chest, "this morality. This intimacy with justice. I had such a heart once, but now…" She sighs.

The children take hammers to locked drawers, tear into envelopes, climb trees and hang off branches to check the roofs of houses. They are suspicious of floors, of walls, of all explanations of innocence. They rope skittish citizens to chairs, leaving them no form of protest except to buck and topple.

"Envy," the father goes on. "The little ones have no understanding of envy. Isabella was immoderate. Too much grace. Too blatantly imperturbable. But she is young. This is why, all my life, I have tried to be neither strong nor rich. Never have envy upon you. With eyes come ill fortune. And never boast. But they shall learn. Just as we did."

Once these young devotees of Isabella's find the plunder (one of the robbers had dropped a vial of Isabella's unmistakable perfume), they maraud through the stubborn door and pour one by one through the windows, and, with their sheer quantity, stamp the two men to the ground, pinning them to the floor in the pool of her staggering perfume. The children scold the robbers, slap their faces, utter incomprehensible things with their mice-like voices, while the two men beg for clemency. The children crush eggs onto the robbers' chests, slop jam into their beards, and douse their mouths and noses with honey and then wine so that the robbers whinny and buck for breath and cough up the sloshing wine.

Lifting the men's beards, the children work a pair of kitchen knives through their necks, and, utterly drugged with the righteousness of their action, they leap along the midday streets of Baraffo, past parents with their mouths open, taking turns hoisting daggers thrust through the robbers' beautifully scented but severed heads.

The people of Baraffo deal with this calamity in their customary way: by never speaking about it. So all abhorrent things dry from their memories, and their minds hold only pleasing memories and, where heinous ones once existed, shadowy creases.

Emboldened by their morning success, the children rededicate themselves to a new purpose: they chant for Babello's freedom. They bang stones together. They shake low branches. They try everyone they come across. Babello, they chorus, must be with Isabella. By nighttime, their parents have joined them in this appeal.

In the central square, Bhara climbs onto the pedestal of a statue that honoured the town's first incidence of rain. Hanging off one of the droplets, his shirt sleeves rolled up his arms, he rouses the crowd with a vision of city-wide justice. He is about half the size of the statue. "Do you want this town to stand for justice?" Bhara booms. "Or love?" he says, opening his free hand and torquing that word with the maximum derision it can bear. "Love," they all chant. They hop as they say it. "Love, love, love." They pull Bhara down by the hem of his pants and push the dejected aide up the switchback stairwell and across the mayor's lawn. "Love," they chant in front of the mayor's home.

In the basement, Bhara pushes the key into the lock, heaves the prison gate aside and points Babello toward the sound of the congregation.

Mazzu helps the prisoner across the floor. He puts a hand at Babello's back and his other hand against the wall as they go up the stairs.

At the grand double door, they are mobbed. The overwhelmed guards stand aside. "Isabella died," one girl says, pulling Babello by the hand. "She was robbed."

"She became stone."

"There were nine suicides."

"She was a pauper."

Babello looks back at Mazzu, who hands over the mayor's walking stick. Babello hobbles across the lawn. He drinks water from a fountain and refreshes himself as he catches his breath, washing his face and hair and touching his chest to feel his racing heart. The crowd points out a narrow home with a tree rising up behind it, casting seeds onto the roof. He pushes open Isabella's front door and stumbles over the threshold. He crawls to her and leans his head against her stomach. He kisses her wrists and, pulling her hands off his face, kisses them too, stunning her with kisses, planting them over her thighs and waist. She strokes Babello's hair. She pulls his shirt off and feels his new chest. Her nails scratch his beard.

With the rumour of their reunion spreading through the town and cascading through conversations, and with Babello on his knees with his forehead against her stomach, Zuraffi lifts herself to a tree outside their window and sees the reunion. As she steadies herself at a juncture of branches, poems fall from her hands. A thought entrances her. Love, she thinks, is a homecoming, a reprieve from psychic banishment. She elaborates it in poem after poem, striking at the energy of the thought from multiple angles and then from the perspective of time, and builds its implications into a philosophy of progress through life.

Those outside the home grab the wind-driven sheets. The poems fall from Zuraffi, but as her sequence progresses, the poems gain a plaintive hue. Those snatching at them find them off-key. Chasing the day's fading sun, she climbs higher and higher into the tree, away from the lovers who inspired her. Pages tumble. Some fragments blow up the road and loft over the town, others are lost, damp and open in the current of the river, and the initial few are tangled by Babello and Isabella's window while, inside, those two wash and ravish.

The children and the others gathered outside experience a double enchantment: the stirring of love, the act of which, behind the closed door, they can only imagine; and Zuraffi's poems, which fall to them in an errant order. The people of

Baraffo grab at these pieces and huddle over them as she climbs higher and higher, until her tree meets with the branches of another. She grabs her way forward, stepping through leaves while shedding her impulses.

Inside the home, washing, oiling, and sitting to a first meal, Isabella asks about Babello's scars. He picks walnut pieces from a smashed shell. He tries a couple of dates, then tests his stomach with pieces of an orange and a dribbly bite of plum. She medicates his neck and washes old blood from his hair.

Babello's fingers bump down her ribs. He feels as if he's near to her essence, that well in her where spirit must abound and replenish.

She eases herself into the warm tub and leans back on him. His hands meet at her stomach. "How was it worth it, then? I missed you every hour. They thought I was a symbol. They asked me for cures. They wanted blessings from me. They think I'm able to give them these things. And I'm always watched now. Sara even told me to be more plain." She lifts her hand and water streams from her fingers. "Now I'm like a puppeteer. If I lift my hand, strings are pulled and others lift their hands too. They look at me as if I'm still the sky. After I was sick, I didn't even want others to know me. You know me. You can know me. They can have their sky."

Wanting to see her changed body, Babello lifts her and turns her around. He feels her stomach, her narrowed legs, her chest.

In the morning, he still moves gingerly. She washes him, trying again to free blood from skin. Sitting on the edge of the tub, she clips his hair and beard. She rubs him a second time with oil that his dried skin relishes. Bowed against her, he savours her; he wants that familiarity that was once absolute.

"What happens now?"

"I don't know."

"Tell them the truth. Tell them everything. Come back and live here."

She lifts his arms too as she washes him. Her once-poised voice is lighter now, gentler, and she has a singsong timbre that effaces the directness.

He has a slow breakfast, starting with half of a pear, two branches of grapes, water, a cup of tea, then, with his stomach awakened, he reaches for the second piece of the pear and saws at a loaf of bread.

Afterward, they sleep across each other like a pair of vines.

§

In their dedication to Isabella, the people of the town lobby to have Babello's prison term annulled. "Let him stay," they chant, in their now-practised syncopation. "Let him stay." Papa, who often lets the will of the masses orient her decisions, stands aside while saying nothing. Bhara strides away from the town square and retaliates with his hardy pen. Published in the next day's paper is his full-page paean to justice.

If there is an exception for Babello—if we simply cancel our punishment for his confessed and abhorrent crime—the ideals of our town's justice would be forever imperilled. Others like him will believe justice is negotiable. That all one needs to circumvent it is emotional appeal. What would our future look like? If popularity and pleas can deform rules of law, and some people can destroy parts of this town with impunity and continue on with their life, what will our town resemble in five years or ten? What has he himself done to prove himself worthy of the greatest charity there is: clemency? Why let Isabella's illness soften our worthy minds? What respect would our laws compel from people? What safety and peace would we live with? What chaos would we be permitting? Why begin a precedent of breaches?

With that article, a fault line is drawn across the citizens of Baraffo: the protesters in the town square versus the militia of roused pens that write on Bhara's behalf.

After another day, once it is settled that Babello's reprieve from prison will be capped at one week, Bhara pushes forward with another request to the town. He writes a second newspaper article, explaining how the negotiated solution hinges on a town-wide vow of silence. "We can let him remain free for four more days," Bhara explains, "if we all vow to forget about this moment when the law was flexible." The broad-chested chief aide urges the town to vow to never speak of the conditions of Isabella's illness or how Babello's prison sentence was punctured with a holiday—and he models this himself by walking the town's streets with his mouth conspicuously shut.

"After one generation," Bhara writes, "this breach in our law will be forgotten. It will be flushed from our memories. When we all die and the new generation succeeds us, the memory of this hole in our laws will vanish too. No one will remember this terrible moment. It will just take one generation. With your co-operation, our laws will have no taint of partiality. With a vow of silence, our children will never know how we weakened into equivocation, and our town can revert to being healthy and admired."

To verify this contract, Bhara mingles in the town square, questioning the people. What he finds is that for every ten people, only one or two confess that they will speak about the banished subjects. Bhara hurries back to the mayor's house, climbs the stairs, and enters Papa's office with the energy of discovery. He grabs a sheet of paper and graphs a curve. He does some math below the curve. "One and a half out of ten people," Bhara says, "would rebel against the imposed forgetting. So, after two generations, only two percent of the people would remember. And after three generations, only a third of a percent. People will call this Bhara's curve!" He smiles at the page.

"But the residue," the mayor says, pointing at the graph. "A residue will always exist. Your curve will never reach zero. So our laws will be in perpetual peril. Some people will always know you and I have made this concession."

"At the margins!" Bhara shouts. "Only at the margins! The margins don't count. It's impossible to control the margins! Within two generations—maybe three—this disgrace will be behind us."

So, out of respect for the mayor, their elders, and their couple centuries' accumulation of peacekeeping laws, and while Bhara frets about his curve, which will never flatten to a gratifying zero, the people of Baraffo talk around the forbidden subject of Isabella's illness and Babello's reverse conjugal visit, indicating a subversive term with a slow swipe of the foot or solidarity with a slight hop. In this way, the people of Baraffo experience the communal invention of subtext and express what they feel without threatening the town's civic health. Children listen to these conversations, unaware of the enormous freight of meaning that slides past their novice ears.

During those seven days, Babello and Isabella thicken with meals. They move on from mild morsels to dishes bearing fats and encompassing bolder flavours. Their hair and eyes gain a lustre. The old vitality and ambition return to their limbs and minds. At night, as Isabella sleeps, her confusion, that inert amnesia that she still sinks into, occasionally returns. In the dark, she sits up on an elbow and scribbles notes that, in the morning, are riddles to her.

The last two nights of Babello's freedom brim with rebellious festivity. When Babello and Isabella are out together, people reach for her as if she were still stone. They touch her forearm, the lobe of an ear, the hardness of her hip. Some try to pull her into an embrace or hold her fingers. Babello receives a similar interest. People confide their dissatisfactions and hardships. As Babello is turned away and listening, one man pulls at Isabella. She fights him off with a hand pushing at his chin and denunciation issuing from her mouth.

Later that night, a group of seven devotees capture her. She wakes with a cloth over her and when she removes it, she sees a group kneeling around her. She uses gentle manners to extricate herself from their zealotry and walks from their candlelight. She returns to her friends. She and Sara hug. As they hold each other, and they hear Babello and a couple other friends running their way, the sisters trade vows: they will no longer walk alone, they will no longer be absent-minded, they will bathe in secret and they will flatten their voices, reflect all light away, marry quickly, and they will never fail the other.

When they arrive home, there is a man waiting behind a tree trunk to catch a glimpse of them and another on the roof outside Isabella's window, begging for her attention and company.

PART 4

13

s he is escorted back into the cell, Babello puts up no resistance. He makes that walk with his chin down.

Mazzu turns on his stool as he comes into the basement.

The guards pull the gate open half a foot and point Babello to walk through the gap. The gate closes behind him.

The boy takes in the changed man. Babello's hair and beard have some splendour, and the skin of his hands and face is revived too. Babello's chest is fuller. Mazzu walks over and realizes with some surprise that yes, the pleasing scent is Babello. It wafts from him.

Mazzu takes some time before he gently questions him.

"You don't have to drop your voice. You can talk in a normal voice."

The boy nods and tries again, but somehow everything is imbued with the soft edges of consolation.

At night, Mazzu brings the lamp into the basement and tries again. "How did you mourn her? Did they give you time, or did they throw you back here?" Mazzu says the prisoner's name and waits.

"We buried her last night. Her sister and I, with a few friends. This morning, the guards found me in the foothills and walked me back here."

"Where did you do it?"

"One friend wanted to plant a sapling over her, or flowers. They thought it would be a memorable site, something we could cherish and return to. But looking at those branches, I thought, why do that? Why let her be fed on all over again? I kept thinking of the white roots growing in jars she kept above her bed. I asked Sara to plant nothing. Instead, a few of us carried the sapling and planted it farther away, on a sunny patch, and we pushed a boulder over her burial site.

"We stayed up late on our last night together, and she was telling us how our lives aren't fully our own. That we belong to others as much as we belong to ourselves.

"After the drought last summer, I didn't think either of us was capable of dying. After living through that, death seemed impossible. Even now, even how I was a week ago, it didn't seem like it could happen."

The lamp by the boy's feet fails. The boy shakes it and the wick lights in his hands, shining against his neck and chin and illuminating the walls and casting shadows of the grass and flowers. Mazzu rubs his hands. With a gust, the leaves rustle and strain from the bars, and the lamp struggles against that wind. The two of them are intermittently lit.

"How did she die, Bello?"

"People thought she was holy. After her illness, she was given hills of jewellery as tribute. A mound of it was on our floor. You would have been astonished. I picked it up by the handful. It was more than I'd ever seen. But it didn't feel like our life. I told her, let's give it away. In just the one week I was with her, each day people came into our home, some to take pieces of it, others to add to it. They wanted to give to and take from what they thought was divine. We'd come home and they'd come out past us. What did it matter if these things belonged to her or someone else? They were just rocks. I should have taken them and left them in the roads. They needed to be near her, to possess her, and learn from her. Some thought she had come back from death and had an understanding of the cosmos. People wanted to consume all aspects of her.

"Even afterward, by that boulder, people walked up and left their stones there, with notes for her. A sculptor came too and claimed that he made her eternal and that she was more his than ours. He pushed the boulder free and sent it rolling. He hated us all and said what her buried body needed was to breathe. I was sitting by the river, watching the water split around that boulder, when the guards found me and marched me here."

§

With one part of town still coughing in the smoky air, images of Babello, Issan, and Isabella proliferate. Simplified portraits are posted in kitchens and hallways, at coffee stands, on fences, trees, along walls, and inside restaurants. Walking by them, Mazzu stops before these images. Sometimes the boy approaches whoever posted it and questions them. "Why did you pin that up? Who is it? What does it mean?" Mazzu feigns innocence and listens while giving no hint of his proximity to the town's icons. He faces these portraits still and absorbed, his eyes carping at the details and the cloying aura.

One day, the boy comes into the basement and waits while Babello sleeps. As the basement brightens, the man stirs on the old mattress. The joints squeak under him. Babello sits up and rubs his face. "I hear you. How come you're here so early?"

"Eat, Bello. Don't go back to the hunger strike. We're friends now, aren't we?"

"Yes, and you should help your friends live with honour."

"No, you should change for your friends. You should do things for your friends if they ask you."

With his hands clasped behind his neck, Mazzu's thumbs rub the necklace that Giulietta gave him and he wears inside his shirt.

Often, when the boy is far from the basement, he overhears a conversation about the town, or Babello or the mayor, and a realization sparks in him. That argument or thought compels him to hurry back across town, down the stairs and into the green-filtered light. In the basement of the mayor's home, it is late in the evening when the boy returns again with an offer.

"Is there anyone you want me to talk to, Bello? I can send a message if you like. I know there are people who want to speak to you. I'll do you a favour, and in return you can keep eating like you were when you were out. I do a favour for you, and you do a favour for me. You did your act. The town is changing. People revere you. They're treating you like you're a prince. They have your picture up and sing your song. You'll go free eventually. And you'll have power. I can't think of one reason for you to die now. What you wanted is happening. Now you should live to see it."

"One day you'll understand. You should live with honour too."

"I have honour, Bello. It's just my name. My name just doesn't sound honourable. But that isn't my doing. Like you said, do one beautiful thing. You did your thing. When I do my thing, believe me, I'll choose to live."

§

For a few days, the boy toggles between respect for the prisoner's grief and his desire to spring Babello from his lassitude. The boy complains about his work while pushing his tools away from him across the workbench. He asks questions, shares news he's overheard, but nothing draws Babello from the window. The boy perseveres into the evening before he gives up and climbs upstairs.

Hearing the stool scrape over the floor and the footsteps in the stairwell, Babello turns toward the leaves. Looking through the openings between the vines, he sees the boy's empty stool and his ordered workbench. His eyes fall to the trough and the shoots that coil up from it. The stems curl in the air of the cell, lunging for the window and its provision of light.

The absence of the boy and his pattering voice brings the man no peace. Babello pushes himself off the mattress, takes a few steps around the cell, then lies with his hands on his stomach. He rolls onto his side. With his hands tucked beneath his chin, he tries to sleep.

In the week that he was free, the cell became a field. Seeds blew in and sunk into the floor. Wildflowers stand among the ankle-high grass, and bees circle, attending to each plant, nosing their way into their scents. In a corner, stems are slumped over, bent by the weight of bucket-like flowers.

Lacking the will for anything, Babello lies there. When he finishes his water, coughing violently after the last swallow, he reaches his arm between the bars and tries setting the glass on the boy's workbench. He leans forward, his shoulder between the bars, but the glass won't reach the tabletop. Babello takes the scissors from underneath the mattress and tilts them in the light, but those blades are dulled. Even when he wipes them, they give no reflection.

§

One afternoon, an intruder with a beard and rough clothes trespasses into the mayor's home. He pulls open the front door, lets it close behind him, then creeps through the house in search of the jail cell guarded by the rasping snakes he has heard everyone talking about. When Papa turns the corner into the main hallway, the intruder forgets about the prisoner and lunges toward the hated mayor. They grapple, his hands on the mayor's shoulders, then at her throat. He pushes Papa into the wall, stifling the mayor's cries with his hand. She bites the man's hand and yells.

Upstairs, in the calm of his office, Bhara raises his chin. He rises from his desk. With his hands in his pockets, the chief aide leans into the hallway. He hears another sound—a muted bump, and then a strange rhythm of footsteps he can't make sense of. He goes to the stairs, and with his brow furrowed, he goes down them. When he sees the mayor on the floor, Bhara jerks the intruder up by the collar, swiftly subdues him, and carries him off. He throws the intruder at the feet of the distracted guards, who have a meal spread out between them. Bhara jogs back into the mayor's home, searches the hallway and sitting room, the kitchen, and back garden. He calls for her. He checks the basement, sees Mazzu working and Babello at the window, and then he runs up the stairs and finds the mayor's bedroom door locked. He talks through it, conveying to her that the house is safe. Bhara goes back to the front door, locks it with the seldom-used deadbolt, then searches the home. He looks in all corners, peers in all closets, commands empty rooms with his broad voice. Bhara climbs to his office and sits with his door open.

Wholly unaware of the intruder and puzzled by Bhara's urgency, Mazzu walks upstairs, calling for the mayor in high spirits. Bhara leans out from his office with a finger over his lips, dimming the boy's enthusiasm. "Let's be quiet. She's resting."

"She's sleeping? Now?"

"Yes," Bhara whispers.

"But it's the middle of the day."

Bhara nods.

The boy looks at the mayor's shut bedroom door. "She should be outside, facing the protesters. She should be working."

Bhara waves the boy into his office. After that one-sided talk, Mazzu trudges across Baraffo in a doomed mood. For the first time, he meets Giulietta without any gift for her. He doesn't sneak in either: he knocks on the front door, walks past her parents with his head down and without noticing their reproof, and goes upstairs.

He sits on the corner of Giulietta's bed. Her mother follows after him and watches from the open door. Giulietta gets up and closes the door. She waits for her mother's footsteps to eventually retreat, before she returns to the bed.

"If Papa was no longer mayor," he says, "where would I live?"

"Why? What do you mean?"

"If she resigns?"

"Nothing would change. You would live with her."

"Where?"

"She would find a home."

"What if I was disloyal?"

"She isn't like that. She won't punish you. You're hers now." Giulietta crosses the bed on her knees and puts a hand on his shoulder. "Wait, what have you done? What are you doing?" She shakes him. "What have you been doing? Hey, did you do something? Hey? What are you hiding?"

She tries to follow along, but what he says is elliptical, hypothetical, and missing necessary pieces.

Leaving her bedroom, the boy passes by her parents again. Mazzu crosses Baraffo.

In the hallway of the mayor's home, he wrestles with a thought. With his left hand, he feels for the wall and follows it.

That night, the boy sits against the other basement wall so all Babello has to do is lower himself off the mattress to pick up the cards Mazzu shuffles and deals. To help them play, the boy unwraps three of the vines off the cell gate. Mazzu raises himself onto his toes, clutching the bars, astonished by the variety of flowers and the height of the grass. Reaching with his ankle, Mazzu corrals the lamp and drags it over the floor to witness the arbour. The light sharpens against Babello, who shields himself with both arms. Wildflowers lean together. The grass is high and seeding. Mazzu turns and looks at his side of the basement, where, because of the leaf curtain that absorbed the sun, there are only the usual stray strands of grass.

In the morning, those vines the boy unspooled and amassed on the floor are alert again, clinging to the gate and reaching across the cell for the window's light.

The boy wakes near midday, when his bedroom is hot, and he kicks the covers to the floor. Missing his friend, he searches Baraffo until he finds Vullie. "You were supposed to come meet me yesterday," he tells him. "And the day before that too."

"The guards wouldn't let me in. I tried waiting in the forest to go inside after they circled the house, but they saw me and yelled. Then I tried at night too, but they spotted me again and really threatened me."

"Didn't you say you were my friend?"

"They turned me away. There was nothing I could do."

Mazzu shakes his head. "One of them could have gone inside and checked with me or with Papa."

"There aren't exceptions. They said Bhara's instructions to them were final."

"I can speak to Papa, then."

They walk around the house. At the windy cliff, where they have to yell to be heard, Vullie offers Mazzu a sweater from his bag. Mazzu shakes his head and gazes out from the cliff, his shirt snapping with the sea wind, while Vullie throws stones. Mazzu can't hear them plunk in the water. All he hears is wind and his shirt. He watches the repetition of waves, the few sails out in the water. Mazzu kicks stones and, peering over the edge, watches them free-fall off the cliff face. Vullie climbs a tree and yells for Mazzu, but Mazzu ignores him and paces with his hands clasped on his head.

§

Mazzu knocks on the mayor's office door. He goes in, leaving the door open behind him, and notices Papa's bruises. Her hand is bruised too and bandaged. Hearing the boy's knocks, Bhara crosses the hallway from his office and joins them.

"What is it, Mazzu?" the mayor finally asks.

"You said that Babello was the leader of the revolutionaries?"

"Yes."

"How does that make sense? If you were part of their party, why would you make your leader set a fire and sit alone in jail? He couldn't be their leader. He's the one they didn't need. He's the popular one. The one they knew would flare up in people's imaginations. That's why each day you're losing power. You two jailed the expendable one. They decided amongst themselves and worked to have him voted as their leader. Even he doesn't understand. And each day, the real leaders are free and undermining you. You two jailed the scarecrow."

§

Mazzu spends two days pestering Bhara and the mayor with questions, then hurries into the basement and tells Babello that he will be moved to the general prison again.

"When?"

"Bhara just wants you to eat," says Mazzu, still breathing heavily after running down the stairs. "They'll overpower you in the prison. He's afraid of the riots if you die. In the prison, Bhara's given instruction for you to be held down and force-fed. The superintendent is being allowed to hire two people just for that. Bhara wants people to forget about you and go on with their lives. They're going to drag you out of here. Then they're going to beat you and stuff you with foods to keep you living. Just eat and stay here with me."

"When are they moving me?"

"In the morning. Bhara asked four guards to come for you this time. But if you eat, Bhara may leave you here. It's worth trying. That's the only bargain you have left, Bello."

§

In the afternoon, Babello wakes quickly, the block of sunlight following him, climbing like an animal onto his bed and lying on his legs. So he tugs the wooden bed frame over the small meadow to the shady portion of the cell. Later, he awakens and sits up quickly. His stomach churns, the muscles grinding inside him. He coughs up the salty water. He wipes bile from his lips and rests with his eyes closed, then sits up again and vomits more.

Wanting to minimize all movement, he breathes shallowly.

Tomorrow, the hunger striker is to be marched from the basement cell by a quartet of trusted senior guards. The mayor has insisted that Mazzu take time away from the basement. So the boy makes a show of leaving in the evening, appeasing the mayor, and returns once she is asleep and the house is silent. So, while Baraffo luxuriates in much-needed rest, Mazzu and Babello sit in the basement, on their final night together, the vines between them billowing with the pressure of wind.

Babello smells unmistakably of pears. The boy sniffs the scent, then looks curiously at the leaves and smells them. He peers through the greenery at Babello, wondering if it is possible that the prisoner could be secretly eating fruit. When Babello sits near Mazzu, the aroma engulfs him. The boy inhales it again and again.

Night rain falls over the trees and roads, and slides off the mayor's grand roof, nourishing the ground below the broken floor of the cell. The rain blows over the red-roofed town, muting Baraffo's protests, pushing people undercover. With the sound of the rain, the boy sometimes mishears parts of what Babello says. For one last time, the boy absorbs Babello's tales of the three people he speaks of most—Issan, Isabella, and Babello himself. These figures will accompany the boy throughout his life and parade in his imagination.

Leaning his head against the wall, Mazzu listens to the man's slurred speech. Instead of lifting his tongue, Babello blends the end of each word into the next, dragging the previous sound through vowels and silences.

Noticing that the salt has upset Babello's stomach, Mazzu

reduces the amount he spoons and stirs into the glass of warmed water. The prisoner sips the potion and sets it down beside him, his mouth and stomach accepting the dilution that prolongs his strength as he sits amidst broken stone, grass, and flowers.

"There was a dog today, Mazzu. A dog came down here while you were gone. I heard a tinking sound come down the stairs and could hear breathing. I unwrapped a few of the vines and coaxed him to me."

"No, Bello," the boy says, shaking his head. "You've gone crazy."

"A brown coat. Curly hair like you."

"There's no dog. A dog's never come here. Hunger's made you crazy, like Bhara said."

"He walked against the wall. When I gave up calling for him, he came over and looked at me with a wariness that was human. These six days being here again, I've touched nothing else alive. Just plants. Then he was breathing in my hands."

The boy shakes his head. "Let me smell your hand, then."

"And even earlier, there were birds that came here, bothering my sleep. They were squawking at dawn."

"Bhara told you it would swallow your muscles then your brain."

Babello rubs his face. All day, he's been rethinking the path of his life and decisions, and how the many forks of his life have become a single, fated line. "Isabella worried about Issan. She wanted me to confront him. She sensed something in him."

"Issan was grown. He takes the responsibility."

"Before I met Isabella, I was just like him. I thought there was no fairness in life. That even wanting fairness was something to laugh at. Then, because of her, it seemed things were possible. I was struggling free of the person I was, my agitation and suspicion and hatred, and seeing it all as new. I did better in classes, and Isabella was over my shoulder, goading me, coaxing me to reimagine who I could be, telling me I was still weighted by contempt that I had to let go of, and it felt everything could crumble. Isabella already had this skill. Twice every year she was in a play and would reinvent herself. I was evolving in her shadow. It felt like a kind of carnival. I didn't have to just be the person I had been. For the first time, another life felt possible. I felt what it was to trust someone, and to love, and I could imagine a future where I prospered. The nights with Isabella, our breakfast, then blazing through a day's ambitions.

"Everywhere I went, I could feel this change coming. In those weeks, I went out on my long walks, and I would come home without words for what I felt. Some days I was jumping with the sureness of it and lying on the floor laughing at how it was inevitable. I knew it. This mayor was done. This town as we live in it now was done. Maybe it would be two more months, or two more years. But I could feel how close it was. It would be different. We would all be different too.

"One night at a restaurant, after many others had left, the rest of us pushed our tables together. Some people began singing a song with derision, the chorus reminding us of the importance of patience in seeking prosperity. All of us were singing, Isabella too, and she was rubbing my leg under the table while we sang. We flipped that folk song. Ridiculing the chorus that pressed down our minds and instructed us to just wait; deriding the idea of patience as a placation. One of Isabella's childhood friends leaned away from our table and said we were compromising our independence. He would never fully join any group. Despite all that was happening around us, he wouldn't loan his being to anything other than himself. And that self-reliance he bragged about, being snide with us in his arguments—what did it do? What does it amount to?"

"But why burn a building? The change was coming. You were certain, so why do that? Why not let it happen? Why make your life into this?"

Babello holds his stomach as he coughs. He waits for his breathing to calm, then resumes talking over the sound of the rain. "What's the twelfth law? That if you work someone's field for nine years, in the tenth year the portion you worked becomes yours. In the eighth year of people working in his building, the man who owned the Peach Building fired them and wanted to hire people from the encampment. But when those in the tents understood what he had done, they refused his offer. The owner then promised that his building would go idle. He would starve them into submission. Isn't that his right? Your mayor thinks so. You thought so too. And it is lawful. So, the building was empty, without any purpose, while whole families suffered. But he was fine because the profit he had accrued would outlast their hunger. At a last meeting that he called, those in the tents vowed to never work there. And those who were fired also vowed to work only if their eight years' labour was acknowledged by him. Never, he said. He would rather let the floor be overrun with cats and dogs. He didn't need it. He said the building could just sit until they changed their minds. My friends were living in its shadow, looking up at it, feeling like they were nothing compared to it, that their lives were worth less than some heap of wood. So, fine, if it should be empty, then let that part of town benefit by it being a field or a park. Let that terrible thing burn. Three hundred of us agreed that no one should have to see that building again, but no one would do the job of burning it."

"So they voted you to do it?"

"After the third vote, which was close to unanimous, it was decided that I would lead. Weeks went by with the Peach Building idle. I hated that building too. I felt like it held everything terrible about this town. Walking by it twice a day, I told my cousins and some friends that I would be the one to burn it. If that's to be done, it should be done by the leader, right? They said yes, and this would be the spark to bring true fairness."

"I knew it," Mazzu whispers.

"An idle building. We wrote articles, but neither newspaper would print them. So we wrote pamphlets explaining how the owner was unjust and how he himself was flaunting his contempt of the *Sixteen Laws*. We handed these out in the squares and at coffee stands, gave some speeches and tried pressuring the owner to relent. But, citing his freedom, he held his ground. That building houses precisely what I hate. Why should there be a freedom to starve and dispossess and crush people? What's so worthy about this freedom? Why should we protect this freedom? What we agreed was that afterward we would all confess. All of us. Those who had worked in the building, those in the camp, other sympathizers, students, and then our cousins and friends too. Hundreds of us. And then people's parents starting agreeing too. Many hundreds of us. We would flood the town's jail. It could only hold, what, two hundred? What would they do with so many of us? How could they jail us all? And what would it say, to have to jail so many? Imagine if each person in this town had someone they loved in jail. What would that do to the town? It would have to change. There would finally be a reckoning. But afterward, with the Peach Building on fire, and the prison guards searching aggressively for who did it, the others became afraid. Only six people showed up to confess. We were beaten once, and we all stood up again, and then I sent them home. I told them I could confess alone. It was inconsequential where I was for a month or two. They would free me. This was my concession to them. Their concession, in turn, was to dedicate themselves to bringing a better way for this town to be.

"After her illness, in my one week of freedom, while others were joyous, she and I were the only unhappy colours. Neither of us knew how long we had together. We didn't want to waste time in sleep. There was her hair, the colour of coffee, a veil that shook over the only person I've loved. While we danced in a crowd, I was sweating, trying to smile. She whispered to me that it would be fine. How, I wanted to know. We'll get married, she told me. She believed in marriage, and how it could somehow bind us across any form of distance. We traded vows that night with four friends with us.

"You can't marry just like that."

"You can."

"Then it's just words. It's no ritual."

"No, Sara knew about an old ceremony she wanted for herself when it was her turn. It was what used to be done, before the town judged that people were marrying too casually and enforced the five-month process. We weren't given five months. We had a day and a night. One friend led us to a secluded spot by the river. We knotted the ends of a rope and, dropping it into a fire, we kept silent until it was burned. One body. She believed in that. She would believe that she's here with me, now. Afterward, we stood on a bridge and heard the river passing under our feet.

"While I was locked up here, night after night, people were flocking to her. You wouldn't believe it. A man named Hetarre, like how many others, poured his ardour into her ears. Even after I was free, I watched him pleading with her, asking her to bless him. I stood aside while he dropped to a knee. She disliked the servility. It wasn't what she wanted for people. She hated that she had somehow caused it. Hetarre spied on our wedding, then climbed a tree to our window and staggered around on our roof, pleading for her. I tried pulling him in, but he was drunk and gesturing with one arm up, and while he was looking back at us, he walked right off the edge. Neither of us could understand. They thought she was a god."

"Was it really you who burned the building? You didn't just take the blame?"

"I ran across the floor of that building. It felt as if I was within a lit rose. The Peach Building was coming apart around me. Fire on both sides of me. I ran the length of it and was trying to find a way out. I ran upstairs, found a barrel, and followed it through a second-storey window." Babello lifts his arms. The sleeves of the prison shirt fall down to his shoulders. He shows his unscarred arms to the boy. "I left it all strangely clean."

14

The boy tiptoes in the upstairs hallway. With the mayor asleep, Mazzu steps into the darkness, shifting his weight carefully over the floorboards. He pulls open a drawer and searches through a mountain of keys. He takes one that is tied together with two others and lifts all three, silencing them with his other hand. He backs out of the bedroom without risking the noise of closing the drawer.

Back in the basement, Mazzu tells Babello there is a gift on the floor. "See if you can reach it," the boy says. Then, trudging upstairs, Mazzu gives in to his grogginess.

Babello pushes a hand through the thicket of leaves and gropes the floor. He reaches between different pairs of bars. He feels something and drags it into the cell. Babello opens the box. Within it, cradled in a piece of leather, are three keys. Babello tilts the box lid toward the light, rubs his thumb over the carving of a boulder, wavy lines of river, and stick lines of a forest's trees that the boy engraved into the lid. Babello plays with the imperfect lid, pushing it open and shut, his thumb on the boulder.

Babello guides each key into the lock of his cell's gate until one of them catches. He uncoils the vines, massing them on the floor. Stepping around them, he pushes against the metal gate. He tugs uselessly at the weight of the iron snakes, then bangs his head against it. He shakes the unlocked gate and screams.

He tries again, bringing his full force until the metal scrapes a few inches. Wriggling, he makes his way through. Babello feels his way up the basement stairs. In the kitchen, he pockets bread and fruits. He drinks water, tasting it curiously, swishing the freshness in his mouth. He rubs water over his face, the back of his neck, and into his hair. Remembering the boy, Babello eases back down the stairs. He pushes the gate over its rails and leaves the box under a rag at the back of the workbench.

Babello passes by the pair of guards, who sit in morning prayer. He ambles across the lawn. With the dawn air clarifying, becoming red then yellow, he takes the steep, wooded path down. In the town, he passes by statues, then walks along the river and past another statue—this one of the town's first merchant of good repute, weighing grapes.

Babello crosses a bridge, arching over boats tied up and bumping in dark water. Mice and birds scatter before him. He passes vacant coffee stalls, the structures desolate without their commerce. He passes restaurants and arrives at a street of homes and, from the pocket of his prison pants, he pulls some of the bread. He waves away several orange-beaked birds that swoop close by, then tosses the bread. Amongst a flutter of wings, some of those birds ravage it before it can even land; others stay and bother his hands, searching him for more prizes. Those birds come down occasionally and, grabbing Babello, they lift him. His legs cycle beneath him. He waves them away and thuds the few feet back to the dust.

People who have ventured outside early rub their sleepy eyes and watch him without recognizing the clothes he wears.

When he reaches a fountain, Babello rinses blood from his shoulders.

He finds a shed and bangs his weight on it and falls through the door. Inside it, he finds a coarse bag, tears it, and trades his prison shirt for this wrap. He clears a spot in the shed and catches his breath. The sun falls through the slatted walls, lighting the dust he heaves in and out of his lungs. As he leaves the shed, stumbling into the brightness of morning, those birds lift away the cloak.

He shuffles across the awakening town. When they bother him, he swats the beaks away.

In the streets of Baraffo, the houses around him are awake, and their coffees and breakfasts are underway. They saw at yesterday's bread and spoon sugar into coffee cups. When the townspeople spot him from their windows, their stares linger. Some turn away absently before wondering about the peculiarity of the pursuing birds. Those whose mornings are fantastical, dreamy, an extension of the wilderness of sleep, stare from their windows with a hand propping their head.

Some people follow him. The group walks in unity, with newcomers assuming its pace and hushed mood. The bravest followers walk at the front of the group, only twenty feet behind Babello, under the cloud of white-winged birds and in its shadow. The cautious hold themselves to the rear or the fringes of the group, where they have room to run off. More and more people open their doors and join the murmuring horde. Some arrive mid-breakfast, bringing a coffee, others in their nightclothes or clothes they hurriedly jumped into.

When the birds swoop for him, the crowd scatters at the edges. They regroup and cling to each other, unable now, despite the danger, to separate themselves from the spectacle. They follow him at a steady distance as though he pulls them with a string. Babello plods uphill toward the edge of the town and the encampment there.

With the noisy crowd pursuing him, he leads them around corners and down lanes while the birds tear strips from his back and shoulders. Blood pours.

The procession gasps as the buzzards carry him over a house. They fly with Babello in their clutches until he beats them off his shoulders; when they release him and he falls the few feet to the street, he is alone, rocking with pain, his head bowed, his blood staining that patch of earth.

Assuming he has disappeared and escaped into the air, the people of Baraffo stand silent, clutching each other, steadying themselves against the chest or shoulder of another, their fingers threaded together. Only some are able to utter hoarse cries; few are willing to submit what they saw to the vainglory of their tongues. Before dispersing, they look around, wondering who they grasped on to at that moment, whose arm gave them that brief and wanted shelter...

Three schoolgirls stand in the road. While the pilgrim gives in, lying down on a road, one girl removes her jacket to spread over him, the second restrains her, and the third steps back as she scans the sky.

§

With their muscled necks, a couple of the buzzards tug at the body and drag him across the road. More of them plummet and bite into his legs. They lift him, his skull and arms hanging loosely. With the town smelling of coffee and the bright smell of puffing bread, and with the sun rising over the sea, the buzzards lift Babello. A woman freezes at a sink when he floats by her window. She is hollow-throated, unable to find speech, wanting to call her children, but also unable to leave that window frame. The bent-necked buzzards struggle. They carry him between trees. When the buzzards bicker, his body falls through the air before others swoop down and clip into his flesh. The people of Baraffo lean from their doorways, use newspapers and arms and their plates to shield their eyes and squint into the harsh light.

Some children, running and jumping in the shadow, follow the flight and heap petals into the air. While they dizzy the air with colour, a boy jumps for one of the low-flying buzzards, capturing it by a wing. Boy and bird tumble through the dust, squawking at each other, each vying for the other's neck, before he splits the bird's ribs against a rock. He catches a second buzzard and pushes it into a rock and sits with his knees on the pinioned, pulsing wings. His friends pull him back by his shoulders, restraining his bloodthirst. The bird, with its neck sunk below its spread gold-fringed wings, flies into the group, brushing them to the ground.

The shadow of their flight passes over benches, hedges, a bend in the river, patches of nurtured vegetables. People duck out of the way of the hanging feet of the man carried across town.

A messenger in overalls is dispatched from a coffee stand. He bicycles across Baraffo to Bhara's home, runs inside, and finds Bhara in his office with a tidy stack of papers, a workable plan for his crucial morning, a single banana, and a mug of coffee positioned on the desk in front of him.

"Bhara, Bhara!" the messenger cries, as he bursts through the unlocked door of the chief aide's home office. "The prisoner is escaping." He pulls Bhara's sleeve.

Bhara readjusts in his chair with open annoyance at the interruption. "Which prisoner?"

"Babello! He's escaped. He's free."

"Babello? Escaped? No," Bhara finally says, leaning back in his throne of skepticism. "Impossible. Impossible."

The breathless messenger pulls Bhara's arm until they're outside. Bhara's eyes follow the messenger's pointed finger, and he squints into the sky. Bhara scowls. He uses a hand to shield the sun. What was that? Forgetting his open front door, the mayor's chief aide drifts across his lawn, then eases into a half run.

Bhara loses sight of the shadow when it disappears behind a home. He goes in a gentle run down the street, cutting through an alley between homes. He springs his body over a shaky fence, and turning out into the street, he sees the silhouette of the birds and their wide-armed prize.

Bhara kicks over a bicycle and kneels and collects some stones. He notices the fallen bike and, with the rocks cradled against him, hops on it and steers with an arm, wobbling across town. When a crowd blocks his way, he jumps from the bike and runs with the rocks. He shouts his way through groups. They break their circles for the majestic chief aide. As he closes in on the birds, Bhara hurls the stones, one after the other. The rocks arc past the target's steady flight. Bhara chases the buzzards through the town, ignoring epithets that taunt him.

Bhara runs through a park and dips doggedly in and out of it and through the empty marketplace, trailed by a number of his students and admirers. People around him begin to clap, sing, stomp, and exhort the buzzards. Others climb onto benches, ledges, and the pedestal of statues to effuse over the prescience of Babello's spirit. Bhara does not have time to stop and challenge all of them. Babello's reputation has become grossly embellished; he hasn't even written much, so his merit and renown rest on conjecture and gossip. Besides, why do people venerate symbolic achievements over beneficial, incremental change? What weakness inhabits people that makes them lard their mind with fantasies?

As he trails Babello, Bhara admonishes the prisoner for the kite-like escape. With the stones he keeps stopping to collect, he tries to knock Babello from the sky. Bhara abhors the impropriety of the scene around him and the speakers who are already making this event into a monumentality. "The monumental," he says disdainfully. He has theories about that class of intellect. The chief aide rationalizes as he runs, the teeth of his mind gnawing at the improbability of this event, and wonders if the prisoner strapped rotting meat to his arms and body to invite the flight. Bhara passes under people who stand on a sagging roof. He tears through rings of chanting people, using his arm to divide them. Some groups cheer and sing their anthems of triumph when they see him. Two parents, fearing the birds, kneel to tie weights to the wrists of their lightest child.

§

In the crowd around the mayor's home, Bhara glimpses Mazzu.

"How does this happen?" Vullie asks Mazzu, who is pale and silent. "What are we seeing? How does a grown man get picked to be carried away?"

"I need rocks," Bhara says, approaching the boys breathing heavily. "Mazzu, help me." In his frenzy, he collects rocks the size of his palm. Bhara's shirt is still tucked in, and he hasn't given in to the indignity of an open sweat.

"How does this happen?" says Vullie. "Nothing can be the same after this."

With many buzzards clutching at him now, the prisoner's body rises. The birds trade his weight between them, and they open his remaining flesh. Babello's blood falls like red snow across Baraffo.

Some people tuck themselves under trees or awnings, until he is lifted above the height of the homes. Others hurry over hills and down roads, tracking the sight. They climb the posts of trellises, they sit atop fences, lean from balconies, and throw down keys to passing friends, who run up. The rooftops of the town teem. The people line branches, straining the wood of old trees.

Men who haven't yet dressed hear the excitement outside and, anticipating a day's festivity, find their brightest and loosest shirts. A child climbs through his window and watches the flight from linked rooftops, stepping across them, roof to roof. An elderly man who has interrupted his solitary morning prayer weeps because he has never seen anything like this before. Another child, lacking expression, does somersaults over a lawn. With one finger, a mother lifts her daughter's chin to the sky, but the child is so young that she finds the straps of her new shoes to be more extraordinary and sets her eyes on those darling replicas.

Bhara passes a man who has climbed onto a statue's pedestal to deliver an oration. The speaker steadies himself by hooking his arm around the figure's stone elbow, and he speaks in a billowing manner, connecting what the people are witnessing to what he knows of history, jurisprudence, and the faint art of dying. He spreads this mythology like a quilt over the shoulders of the fifteen people who ring him. "This is a vindication of the meek," he says with his drying throat. "We can strike back, and we will be protected. This world is ours to make of it what we will."

"Error! Error!" Bhara cries.

One woman pleads with those nearby to turn their hearts against the rising influence of Zuraffi. Now, she says, isn't the time for philosophy and complexity. It is the time to bluntly say what is needed. If Zuraffi lacks the courage to do so, we should build a fence to stop her from encroaching on our hearts.

Bhara's decency is intact, his shirt has not come untucked, and he thankfully put on good pants this morning. What he needs is to catch the buzzards before they reach the sea, before they have a clear path to the cliff-edged island where they eat and breed. He runs past another man speaking from a pedestal, this one linking the prisoner's flight to a far-flung and theoretical notion of oppression. "When long hours of labour and injury are not enough, they give us bars; when bars are not enough, they give us lies and stones!"

"God!" Bhara cries. If only there was enough time to sit and correct them!

Bhara runs across the bridge. He throws one of his rocks. Seeing it pass under the dangling man, he resumes running. Many buzzards are gathered now in the air. They sweep Babello higher into the fabulous blue, dropping him for a moment then grabbing him again and carrying him toward the clouds. Babello's skin tears, his flesh buckling and bunching in their gnarled claws. They raise him into the crosswinds and the curved beaks tug strips of meat off him, so as they fly their cargo becomes lighter and lighter. The birds swallow a portion of him, another portion falls and embeds itself in the town, his blood streaming into soil and aquifer. They unravel the bones from his parcel of flesh. Small ones slip free and clink against the red roofs and roll off them and into the lawn—with a single step they are lost, forever pushed into the soil. One by one, his fingernails flutter free. After the tiny bones of his body fall, the trophy bones are next. They break windows and spin in the streets—people leap from the hazard of these falling objects, then wrestle for them. The hipbone. The immaculate bone of a thigh that swoops through a tree, shearing leaves and scattering the witnesses who perch there.

The people leap and push each other off the branches as the pieces of Babello sprinkle over the town.

With all the noise and pushing, Mazzu loses Vullie and makes his way into the mayor's home. The boy retreats to the basement. Alone and overcome, he fiddles with the wooden box he finds on his workbench. With his hands on his head, he faces the locked cell.

Giulietta, having glimpsed him sneaking through the crowd, hurries after him. She does a full turn on the mayor's lawn. Charmed by the majesty and proportion, she lingers for a moment. She neatens herself as she climbs the steps. The guards, recognizing her and aware of the status of her parents, stand aside for her. Giulietta searches the ground floor. She walks through the sitting room, then the sun-filled kitchen. She climbs upstairs, finds the doors locked, except one whose knob turns. She pushes open Mazzu's bedroom door, recognizes a shirt of his over a chair, and absorbs the regimented arrangement of the room. One wall has pencilled drawings taped to it. She opens a closet. She touches the guitar case and wonders why he has never mentioned that he plays. She adores music…it transports her.…She bends to look out his window. There is no mirror in the narrow room, and no books either.

She goes back downstairs, and finds another, dim stairwell. She descends the crooked stairs slowly, with both hands against the walls. The scent of a garden puzzles her. She turns into the light and sees the workbench and array of tools and, behind the snaking bars, the floral cell. The boy sits on the floor.

"What are you doing?" She holds her hands out. "It's amazing. Come. Come watch the flight with me." She pulls him to his feet. There is a broken wooden wing fastened to the wall above his bench. This area has all the curious minutiae and personal feeling that his bedroom lacks.

He follows her bounding ankles until they are outside together. Her arms surround him in the sunlight. "Look," she sighs. With her lips at his ear, the boy is connected to her breaths. "It's an actual miracle. This isn't Gaspo. This is life."

§

Holding three rocks, Bhara runs down the hill, skidding wildly on one foot, and sees the water crashing against the coast. "Move, move, move!" he cries, running without control. The wooden dock pitches under the weight of Bhara's strides. When he is halfway down the dock, Bhara leans back and fires the last rocks, one after the other. The first and second throws miss the birds. The last stone passes between buzzards, shocking them. They flutter and squawk. The body cartwheels, only a few birds clutching it now. The stones plunk one after the other into the distant sea. The last couple of birds release their prize.

From the high ground of the mayor's home, Mazzu squeezes Giulietta's arms against his stomach as the gnawed remains of Babello fall end over end. He looks away. He turns around in her arms.

People run by Bhara and jump off the end of the dock, splashing into the water. Regaining his breath, Bhara looks down between the planks of wood and watches the water heave beneath him. Very faintly, he hears the ocean take the prisoner's body.

People engulf Bhara. Shedding their clothes as they run down the hill, they dive into the morning water—some grab at Bhara and try to take the fully dressed man into the water with them. Bhara flings them aside.

The swimmers search for the last shreds of Babello's remains. They tunnel into the water, peer around in the dark, then rise to the surface and wipe away the veil of water, hoping the body bobs near them. People continue jumping from the dock. They vanish from each other as they swallow air and kick their way as far beneath the surface as they can before streaking back toward the light. They rise empty-handed, bursting for air. Climbing out, they bask on the golden shore.

Those prone to worry prop themselves on an elbow. "Are you going to work today?" one man asks, then turns the other way. "Are you?" he asks. "Will I be fired if I don't?"

"Fool, God just came down and plucked our brother to be with him up in the sky—of course there's no work today. Today we do what we want."

With townspeople rushing by him, Bhara walks down the dock. Already, the storytelling and flourishes have begun. The people gather and debate the number of birds, the origin of the journey, the meaning of the route, the necessity of paddling out to that island where the buzzards breed, and gut feelings they had on waking and opening their eyes. They braid what they saw with personal whims and omens. They trade their whereabouts when they realized what was happening, argue over which of the town's hills gave the best vantage point, compete over who was the first to witness it, and learn from each other what happened when their vision was blocked. "It was the clouds. Once he reached the clouds, they couldn't carry him beyond it. One must not rise above clouds. That is the truth to learn. That is the wisdom here. We have limits we should respect."

"It wasn't the clouds, it was the tax man's rocks."

"No way he could throw as high as the clouds. He isn't half the man I am, and I could not throw anything to the clouds."

In a town-wide jubilee, the people of Baraffo wreath each other with kisses. They share what they know of Babello, his sacrifice and instructions for the town, and what they themselves should do. Those loyal to the mayor stand aside in equivocation as balloons loft in the air and the town's wedding cannons are stuffed with heaped-up flowers and fired one by one, scenting the sea and the shoulder-to-shoulder swimmers. They climb out at the shore and embrace each other with a tingle, an importance, a gravity. Though life is indeed brief and mean, they smile at the realization that it is still, perhaps, something of unparalleled worth.

Bhara walks by people who have pushed their barbeques out into the park. They delegate cooking assignments. Knives impale onions, eggplants, tomatoes, and piles of peppers. Famished from swimming and chasing the body across the town, townspeople sit with boards in their laps and help slice up the day's feast. Wheelbarrows of potatoes arrive. They are tipped over and sent rolling away for more. The people season the meat, brush the vegetables with oil and lay them over the grills. Though it's still morning, Baraffo begins an impromptu festival.

"I don't know what I was doing," one open-shirted man roars while tending a barbeque. "But I know I was sullen! Now, look at me, I am man of the hour."

"You're always sullen in the morning!" his wife cries.

"And now, I am saying, I am a wonder of the world."

Walking over the crest of the hill, people hug Bhara's colossal figure. He studies the surroundings from the hilltop, and walks away from the guitar players who combine melodies in the shade of trees. Bhara doesn't know these people, doesn't much like them, but submits to the affection of their arms. They hug him and pull his neck so they can kiss his shaved cheeks. He trudges uphill, past the littered clothes, to the mayor's home. He passes by orators speaking in dramatic tones to hushed audiences. Bhara walks over to the park and searches the grounds and shadows and benches for his wife. He can hear some of the town's statues smash against the ground. Bhara frowns as the town's monuments, that irreplaceable tribute to its preciously strange history, topple from their perches.

The people of the town chant revolutionary songs.

Bhara passes through the marketplace, peers into his home, and calls for Katrina. Alone, he climbs the wooded hill back toward the water, presides over the clothes-strewn hill, and turns to the refuge of the mayor's home.

Using their newspapers as plates, people invite Bhara over to join them. "I have been suspicious of these birds for many years now," one man says, with a finger raised. "They are always around. I don't like the way they go around and around, circling above me—and their disgusting heads! I have never turned my back on them! Never! We should have far fewer birds around. And I gladly eat chicken. People ask me, 'Do you feel guilt?' I never, not once felt any tinge of guilt about eating something so horrible."

Bhara is sure that life, truly meaningful life, is for the serious. The others, those undisciplined, wind-blown ones, skim sensations off the top. Bhara walks from hill to hill, patrolling the carnival. *Absurd*, he thinks, seeing all the damage: statues shattered, hefty branches lying across roads, roofs caved in.... He overhears that the main bridge has collapsed and the river thrashes through the wreckage. Everywhere he looks, he tabulates the tax that would be needed just to restore the town. He knows people will revile his former colleagues who will come knocking for the money. To think, all the good that was inscribed into the town could be undone just like that. It is as though, he thinks, all those stars arrayed above, which he has studied with awe, instead of wringing their glow with their birth's noble obligation, were laughing their light. Appalled, Bhara rubs his head. *Yes*, he thinks, recollecting the midnight observation he has made on countless occasions: *the starlight does falter. They twinkle. They laugh at us.*

From the dock, people dive into the seawater. Bhara observes their games and splashing and flirtation. Baskers spread themselves over the shining rocks and drowse, and Bhara hears lewd sounds from the bushes. From the height of the mayor's hilltop, he sits on a bench and watches the town's rapture.

"We are never alone," the man who is on the pedestal of a statue shouts. He notices Bhara and raises his voice to lure the chief aide into debate.

Bhara looks across the scene, from one side to the other. Who is making the town better? Who is buttressing its best aspects? "I hate all of you," he says, waving his arm across the whole town.

Children pass him, running down toward the water. The swimmers who climb out onto the shore glance back with envy at the giddy fish. When they recuperate, they find the fishermen and persuade them to push out into the waves to search for the last missing remnants of Babello.

§

The chief aide goes into the basement. With his face and arms tinted green by the leaves, he inspects the arbour. Bhara unlocks the gate, heaves it, and sits on the mattress, which springs up on either side of his weight. Searching the cell, he finds scissors under the mattress. He examines them, fiddles the lock with them, and sets them on the windowsill. He crouches, gazing under the bed frame and feeling along it. He picks up some of the broken stones of the floor, interrogating them with his hands, as if they could have been complicit in the escape. He pushes against the ceiling stones then tests the bars of the window.

Bhara gazes out of the window, flips through the couple of fantasy books the boy brought down for the prisoner, then searches the boy's workbench. He opens the drawers and fishes with a finger through jars that hold a chisel and nails. He rummages through the pile of scrap wood. Bhara circles the cell, as though this activity would yield the tactic of the man who was locked up here.

He has a thought and measures his thickness against the gap in the bars.

When the mayor comes down the stairs with a chatty prison guard, Bhara is standing in the garden cell. The mayor's eye is still bruised. She sees Bhara and sends the prison guard away.

"It was locked."

"How did you get in?"

"Your key. From upstairs."

"You went into my room?"

He nods.

Papa sighs. "Come, let's have a drink together."

"No. I don't want to go outside today."

"Come upstairs, then."

The mayor pauses there, absorbing the wilderness. Plants even grow from the walls, from the fissures in stone where there are narrow beds of soil. Her arm is outstretched, beckoning her chief aide.

"No one was helping me," Bhara says. "No one. They spoke to me as if I were the villain. I'm more hated than an arsonist."

"Come. Get up."

"Not one person. No one. I was alone. Where were you? Even my wife. Where was she? We should have all been censuring him. I work here serving the town, and he damages it. I serve you honestly. I'm always true with you. But people would rather be a part of destruction."

"I know, Bhara."

"You should hear the names I was called."

With the mayor's arm over Bhara's back, they walk toward the stairwell. The mayor glances over her shoulder at the flourishing cell and sees the trough, some ripped vines that hang off the grill, and the enclosed meadow.

Bhara slumps at the kitchen table.

"We will have to come up with a plan," Papa says. "If we have any hope, it will be in convincing people that we commissioned the birds. That they had our blessing."

Bhara lifts his chin and looks at the mayor, who is in her usual mode of garrulous good humour.

"Or," she says, "we step out of the way and let this town renew itself without our guidance. We have a day or so to decide. After that, the decision will be made for us." Papa finds a jug of wine and two glasses. She pats Bhara's shoulder. "If we decide to, we could say it was under our auspices." She pulls out a chair. "We could say we prayed for the birds to help us resolve our impasse. It was the only way out of this. But Bhara?"

He lifts his head.

"Something wondrous happened. And we were able to see it."

"Don't you see? I failed you," Bhara says. "I failed. You trusted me. Radicals didn't bring you down. It was me."

PART 5

15

Just ten years later, it is difficult for the people of Baraffo to interpret their town's awakening. The competing accounts often indicate an author's bias more than a commitment to history. Even the crucial names shift, their personalities seemingly drawn in sand, so that each new account washes over their portraits, leaving them increasingly vague. Those in the town who stop and stare at the statues honouring the brothers who lit the fires discern little of their identities. Their stone faces are idealized, without depth or specific character. Neither pedestal bears a name. Neither statue bears Issan's sour eyes or the scar across his cheek, and neither bears Babello's posture or physiognomy.

The statues are positioned opposite each other so that the people of Baraffo can walk between them, the sculptor revealing how at sunrise in the spring, the shadow of the older brother reaches over the road and touches the stone shoulders of the younger brother. At sunset, the younger brother repays this gesture, his shadow climbing to the elder brother's heart.

The town's historians study the awakening and quarrel over their findings. They crowd together atop this subject, jostle for prominence, and dedicate their lives to their interpretations.

Some charge that the mayor was a puppet propped up by wealthy loyalists. They use some of her decisions as evidence of a pattern of favouritism.

Others who lived well before the revolution and whose status suffered because of it become obsessed with what they lost. These people consolidate their decline into songs exalting the town's pinnacle and grieving its vanished glory. They celebrate their past as uncorrupted, a golden age without hardship, when they were free and innocent—a time when friendships prospered and the full delights of love were possible. These songs celebrate how the town's orchards once struggled under the burden of their fruit. In these fables of abundance, the breaking of a branch is described as an act of mercy to the tree. These loyalists to the mayor feed each other melons before joining hands and circling in dance, stomping, raising up the dust, and chanting at the sky. It pleases these once-prosperous townspeople that the town's name remained unchanged through the years, giving them hope that their precious garden is not eternally lost. Baraffo will revert, they promise, to its splendour. They make it their private mission. For them, even voicing the name is a portal to paradise. *Baraffo*.

One historian is vilified by those who were rich because his account has no elegiac tone. He notes that "oppression is most insidious when it is carried out patiently, by civil people, in dignified clothes, with the feeling that what they are doing is just."

Taken together, these responses, compiled in the years following the awakening, comprise an anthology probing the town's hot-tempered past.

One document rainbows across the town. Students are obliged to read it, many memorize parts of it, and it is accepted as one of the awakening's fundamental texts:

The preludes to our awakening are infinite. I could write that it came like spring: inevitably, with bluster and dark clouds, and, despite the violence, with optimism. It was predictable: we could feel it, but this did not diminish the courage or confidence we had. We stepped from the shadow of subjugation and saw a new way. We stopped and wondered, why now? Why would this happen only one season after the catastrophe of drought? But what must be remembered is that because of the drought, it felt like nature itself was on our side. Nature was the lead rebel. Nature was our commander. This is who we followed.

We were exhausted and hopeless. But how does squalor explode into an uprising? A first answer is this: the day of the second fire, when the Plum Building was burning, and while Babello was silently rousing us all from a hilltop jail, this second fire was our uprising. How many times must people be awoken? For us, it took three shoves. It was a year zero. We were reborn, with neither a past to take pride in, nor a future that included us. So, we threw our lives away.

We stole. We obstructed. We painted messages over every-thing. We planted vegetables in the lawns of the hilltop rich. We pitched tents in their gardens. We trespassed and slept in their homes. We took their clothes and wore them. We sat with and amused their children. We forced ourselves upon them as exiled brothers and sisters and made them see us. And we became great-hearted. During meals, we pulled a chair to their table and helped ourselves to potatoes, corn, a basket of bread. We defied the boundaries. The only protection we had against laws and customs was our attitude, which was cer-tain and kind.

But there is a second answer to this question. In this, I paraphrase a friend and our night-long talks. Our thought is this: there is no paradise. This town is no paradise and never was. Paradise is built upon injustices we avoid seeing. This is the function of the word, to draw a curtain and keep suffering from our eyes. The unfairness of this town was no accident. The unfairness was the purpose.

So, why now? Why us? Where did our great-heartedness come from? Why did it not come earlier, and save my parents or grandparents from their life? From the eastern shore to the western foothills, it was a jubilee. Some have said the awak-ening came like spring, or dawn, or like a river that flows into the sea, but even though the events deserve grandiosity, these embellishments are gross.

How did it happen that this generation, people with the usual courage, people you would even find meek and submis-sive, resigned and disgraceful—how did we awaken and fight? How does meekness become fire?

We were told to be patient and reasonable. All things, we were told, improve with time. We were told with patience we would all be equal. We were told to be grateful. We were told to be good. We defied this, rejected it, and changed it.

The town's historians can race each other to the source of our uprising, but our awakening was an act with many causes. Each family, each of us, had our own reason to embrace jail or injury. Our misery defies a single reason. So, we should shed our colour and grandeur and say simply that "the revolution came."

The chronicles establish that it was the Peach Building that was burned first, then the Plum, the twin manufacturing buildings named for the tint of their treated wood.

The mayor spent her influence tamping down the significance of the first fire. The second fire burned above her exhausted authority. She shuffled through her house with a self-doubt that was new to her, while other fires burned in the town's hearts.

PART 6

16

The boy faces the trough and the vines smothering the gate. Mazzu walks in a circle. He tears some of the vines and carries them to the back garden. He comes back with a bucket and piles the vines into it. He carries it outside. When the boy comes back down, he has a shovel. He fills the bucket with soil from the trough. Unable to lift the full weight, the boy transfers some of the soil back into the trough. He carries it up the stairs, setting it down whenever his hands and shoulders need relief.

Mazzu pulls nails from the grip of the wood and sets them on the workbench and leans the planks against the wall. The trough comes apart in his lap. He wipes his forehead with his shirt. He takes the last tray of food that was left for Babello up to the kitchen and rinses it clean. He washes his face and scoops water into his hair, cooling himself.

Without the vines, the basement is luminous, and a breeze passes over his bare arms. He sweeps the leaves and spilled soil and pieces of the crumbled floor into a pile; all these relics from the past months he sweeps into the bucket and dumps outside in the garden behind the home.

On his stool in the restored basement, he leans back against his workbench. Mazzu pushes his hands through his hair and moves the nails away from the centre of the bench.

He takes his glass of water and sits on the floor. Gazing at the flowers, their colours and shapes and slant, the boy slumps into sleep. When he wakes, he's against someone. He has a confused, sleep-mangled conversation with Giulietta, who has defied her parents and insisted on staying with him. She breezed by the guards, checked his bedroom, and then, with her hands against the wall, she descended again to the basement.

"What are you saying?" she says. "You're mumbling. I can't understand."

"He told me everything. I know everything. I know the whole story," the boy says, before his eyelids weaken and he plummets into a sleep saturated with dreams.

Giulietta absorbs the cell, the provision of light, the snakes and their rasping mouths, and the scissors that catch her eye and glint on the ledge. Easing Mazzu off of her, she leans him against the wall and approaches the gate. Her hand passes between the bars and cups a marigold. The lilies, which she loves most, are out of reach. She turns toward the boy's workbench. A letter she wrote to him hangs from a misshapen nail. She touches the bend in the metal. While Mazzu sleeps, Giulietta sits on his stool replaying the conversations they had, and reinterprets them.

§

During the town-wide carnival, Bhara adheres to his daily routine. Once festivities subside, he announces that he will give a lecture aimed at Baraffo's youth.

With the classroom buzzing, Bhara enters from the front door and unpacks papers from a folder. He glances up at the students while he arranges the pages. The students hush and look at him with excitement. Bhara knows the youth of the town are restless and troubled. And though they hold him in esteem, they neither like nor trust him, and he has set himself a personal plan to rectify this. But that morning, as he faces them, there is an air of disturbance in the room that interferes with his usual rapport.

Bhara walks around the desk and leans back against it, panning across the room of students who fill the chairs, the stairwell, and the floor space. Picking up some signal, some feeling from them, Bhara abandons the intentions of his mapped lecture, crosses over to the wing, and tries to pinpoint the room's undercurrent. From their eyes, he senses dissipation and contempt. *They look drained, spent...but what is that charge*, he wonders. *Nostalgia? Is it nostalgia? For more carnival? Longing for what has passed? Melancholy? Is it melancholy? Caused by the significance of the past week?* Even though he tries to suppress it, he reviles the passivity of melancholy. Are they looking back at the wildness of the week with fondness? He looks at the students sitting on the stairwell. Do they feel it was a tragedy? Are their minds so weak?

"Who here is unhappy?" Bhara demands.

The students have heard of his challenges. His approach is known to be unusual. He isn't ingratiating or encouraging, and he doesn't minimize himself to flatter the students the way other lecturers do. Rather, he is forceful, idealistic, and large. They watch him without replying. Some of them write down this first line. With his autonomy emanating from his shoulders and chest and head, they can't tell what direction he will swerve, what path his thinking will take, or what subject matter he will have reached when he triumphs.

In the still air, some students fan themselves with their notepads.

"Who here is unhappy?" he booms out again, waiting for them.

The students look at one another until a couple of arms rise into the air. Other arms rise more tentatively. After minutes of silence, the remaining hands pop up. Twisting in their seats, the students relish their agreement. Bhara waits in the corner, nodding. All of those students, the whole classroom, sit with their arms up. They look at their friends and smile and wink in anticipation of the joy of being split in half by Bhara's rough logic.

"I," Bhara declares, "am not unhappy."

He returns to his desk and collects his notes. He leaves the building and crosses the sunny town.

Bhara refuses to let the week's liberation induce any undue emotion. If students succumb to wayward freedoms, that's their choice, but he refuses to address them while they are in an abject state of mind. Bhara pulls open the door of his home. "I am not unhappy," he says, walking past his wife. "This was no tragedy." He goes into the office.

Katrina sits in the kitchen, reading, her legs up on a second chair. She touches her head and thinks of tapping on his door, then reconsiders. *Bhara is an odd, restless man. Later he will be approachable.* There will be a breeze in the room, and he will eat lunch alone, after her, in his steadying solitude.

Katrina turns back to her book and falls into its questions. She has been lodged in it for hours. She picked it up a few days ago and used it as a refuge from the anarchy of the town, which she didn't feel herself capable of joining. She walked far from the town with that book and sat at a shady portion of the riverbank with it then returned to that same spot the following day. Glancing at his closed office door, Katrina thinks of Bhara's pain—of his inarguable goodness and isolation; no one could deny the virtue of his heart—and she sighs. For now, there is nothing she can do for him.

§

In the early days after Babello's death, Mazzu descends to the basement without wanting to work. He doesn't select a poem from his pile or clamp a plaque to his table. He idles at his workbench for those hours, then faces the cell, wishing Babello were there.

With Giulietta, Mazzu swallows many thoughts as they arise in him. She sees this: a thought rising through him into his expression, his face changing with it, then his mouth opting not to speak it as he looks away. "It's nothing," he says.

These are days when people interested in Babello besiege the boy. They lean down to him and bombard him with questions about Babello's character, politics, his aura and habits. The boy begins telling half-hearted lies, tall tales that surprise whoever is standing close by him. These townspeople fan out through the roads of the red-roofed town with a flock of the boy's stories jostling in their mouths while they search for Babello's treasured bones. Mazzu's fibs decorate evening conversations. The people of Baraffo listen to these accounts with interest until some leap into the air, bothered by the disparities in the stories. They raise their concern until the disputing tales are tugged together, the points of contention reconciled, and the many accounts merged into the likeliest and most consensual truth. A few people, however, distrust these compromises and approach the mayor, asking Papa to compel the boy into a faithful telling. With a wave of her hand, the mayor sends these truth-seekers away.

In the days of reflection that follow the carnival, the citizens of Baraffo demand changes. Some request a barrier to protect themselves from those living in the encampment. Others sketch how the river could, with some work, be used as a moat against them. They petition the mayor and the mayor's chief aide and inundate the more fatalistic newspaper with dismal projections of the town's future. Meanwhile, a larger group of townspeople use the miracle of Babello's prison flight to demand a general evening-out of the town's governance. "Why should we be tiered?" they ask.

"Why should some live while others suffer?"

"How can stealing food be a crime?"

Mobs of people hack down trees that shade the homes of the rich. The rude sunlight spoils those homes, discolouring carpets, fabrics, and paintings.

The protests continue until a town-wide amnesty is granted for bloodless crimes. The doors of the general prison are opened.

Many of the prisoners walk out of the old horse stables in disbelief.

These are days of feuding. Bhara tries to combat the effects of Babello's prison flight. The mayor, meanwhile, is aloof, wrestling with possibilities in a state of long reflection. While the chants in the town square persist, Papa abstains from public statements.

Rallies form in front of the mayor's home. The people meet in the marketplace and march through the roads and climb up the walls of the mayor's house and peer in windows. Many remain overnight on the lawn, asking for a fairer voting process. A newspaper warns of the peril of this endeavour: would the newly released prisoners vote too? Why should they benefit from both amnesty and influence when they have contributed nothing at all to the town? Would newcomers arriving in the foothills have a vote? And what then would prevent Baraffo's precious nature from being overrun and irrevocably altered?

On the fourth day of protest, with a crowd gathering again on the lawn, the mayor sits at the kitchen table with Mazzu. They talk and drink cups of tea together.

Afterward, Papa walks out of the grand house. She goes down the few stairs and crosses the lawn. She raises her arm—this is all she needs to generate the necessary silence. Speaking brightly, thanking those there and commending their devotion to the town, she asks that she remain as mayor for a further month to ensure a calm transition. She proposes a date of election, and explains this request for a final month to the rival newspapers, which both acquiesce, tamping down the unrest into a town-wide tranquility. While she performs this oration, those standing on the grass notice the cut on the hand that she gestures with, and the bruise near her eye.

During the grace period of her month-long exit, she channels the demands of the protesters, implements a ten-member council and an expansive voting procedure, formalizes the Sixteen Laws into a penal code, and adds a seventeenth: that if a law is broken, a citizen forfeits their vote until a proportional restitution is made. The people of the town consider the seventeenth law her final accomplishment. In turn, they grant her the seaside home to live in for the duration of her life. Papa has served them for nearly forty years, giving her life's energy to them. The coastal, wind-battered home is her due recompense. The new mayor would live in the core of their town.

§

Looters break into Babello and Isabella's home and hurry off with mementos. Some are reasonable with what they take: a shirt, a seashell, or a plant. Others pocket dearer items: a stone ring, a painting. Their footsteps leave tracks in the dusty floor. The boy alerts the mayor to these trespassers. Papa jumps up, and the two of them walk over together. They enter the home through the fallen door. Waving her arms and bellowing, Papa casts the looters away.

While she gives instructions and makes a list of who is permitted to come inside, the boy wanders through Babello's home. Mazzu looks through the shelves, opens a wardrobe, and walks out onto the balcony. He absorbs the home's atmosphere. He sits at the kitchen table. As Mazzu is about to leave, a cheaply bound book catches his eye. The boy flips through the opening pages of the homemade book Babello wrote. He slips it under his shirt and keeps it for years to reread.

When he sees Giulietta and she questions him, the boy says nothing. The despair, she understands; being upset, she understands. But she struggles to understand his sudden inability to speak. When pushed, he confesses to her that he feels lost, that he doesn't know who he is. "You're still you," she says. "Nothing that happens changes that." He shakes his head, unable to find an inroad into himself.

§

Months after Babello's prison flight, Giulietta still notices indications of Mazzu's grief. In groups, with his bombast, he can appear normal, unfazed, and quick-witted. When questioned about Babello's hunger strike, he confirms that he never saw the man eat anything save for flags. He thought nothing of eating three, four, in one afternoon, Mazzu answers. But alone with her, he is quiet. He spends entire nights without offering much, so instead Giulietta talks away. In a rare moment, the boy becomes preoccupied with Babello and speaks about him, unaware that to her these memories are wholly apart from whatever she had just been relaying to him.

Years later, when he's eighteen, the boy reads a subset of books, the town's dissident histories. When he reaches passages that argue against Papa's style, he remembers Babello and returns to the two-month period in the basement of the mayor's home when he sat at his bench and the prisoner paced the burgeoning cell, tutoring the boy, laying idea upon idea over Mazzu's undernourished mind.

Mazzu suffers from a recognition: there are tracts that he would likely never have read if he hadn't met Babello, or would have only read glibly while mocking the authors. He thinks of that conceited, parallel self and is disturbed by what he would have matured into. It agitates him that he wouldn't have been able to rely on himself and his own efforts.

Adding it up honestly—the know-how he inherited from Papa, the point of view of Babello, the flavour and pointedness he drew from Zuraffi's verse, and the influences of Vullie and Giulietta—weighing it all, Mazzu believes himself to be a mere collage. Nothing seems inherent to him. It all seems inherited. He struggles to find an authenticity that can withstand his scrutiny.

Even five, ten, twelve years after Baraffo's awakening, Mazzu's thought will bear an undertow, as though Babello still had the power to grab the boy's mind and pull him to his perspective. The boy takes his bicycle and searches the foothills until he finds a mound of overgrown rocks that he walks around and touches. He spots the sapling planted near Isabella's grave and touches the stem and picks a leaf for himself. He goes downhill and finds a boulder lodged in the river and the water parting around it, and clears a spot to sit. He cycles to this spot regularly and builds a rough shelter to take cover from any rain or undue sun.

Days before his nineteenth birthday, Mazzu relinquishes a prized possession. Unlocking the door of the mayor's library, and with its contents and cadences memorized, he shelves the copy of Babello's book. Poised before the wall of spines, with his hand out, he deliberates over what genre to shelve it with. Mazzu wedges it into place on the high shelf of historical accounts and leaves it there, alongside the town's other subjective histories.

Many years later, when the boy's hair is white and bound behind him, and after his own embattled term as mayor has emptied his convictions and exhausted his ambitions, his own contribution is added to the hilltop library. Late in Mazzu's life, with the town still split into feuding enclaves forty years after the awakening, he unites Baraffo's factions with a telling of Babello's life.

Filling his account with exuberance, romance, and beauty, he charms both halves of the population with a simple, overlooked truth: driven by grief from the death of his beloved, Babello found refuge from his worldly pain in the solitude of a garden cell. Mazzu lightens all references to the fires, riots, and hunger, and he even suppresses the figure of Babello and instead lauds Isabella, filling his poem with proofs of her grace and courage and singularity. He describes how, with the help of his brother, Babello climbed a ladder each night to her bedroom window to see her, and he lists the many suitors who died trying to win her heart. Favoured by all quarters of the town, this story becomes Baraffo's favoured myth.

If whole histories can be distilled and shown to pivot on the backs of solitary figures, then it was Babello who knifed the town's breach and the boy, forty years later, who stitched it up and medicated the gaudy wound with a generous dose of lyricism, irony, and joy, while in between them was a two-generation period when Baraffo underwent a bitterly beneficial reckoning. The boy converted Baraffo's death tolls, arson, and pain, into a myth of danger, ideals, and unsurpassed love in which birds gathered to lift a mortal to a more ethereal union with his beloved, and he seasoned his account with eros, humbling reversals, and descriptions that tempted the town's hearts, making it hard to sustain hatred.

The title of that epic, which is long, gregarious, and cumbersome to say in its entirety, became chopped, simplified, and known as *The Legend of Baraffo*. The people imitated it, venerated it, defended it against the perfection of the moralists, and in their conscience, they measured their own deeds against it.

That absorbing myth prompted fantastical statues, lurid paintings, popular songs, a reformed legal code, street names, the names of children, and then dishes in restaurants, customs, holidays, and figurines. The tale itself was multiplied into other languages and tones. Future conquerors found its personality seditious and suppressed it, but after enough time, it bobbed to the surface again, barnacled with the bittersweet horror of excess. That *Legend* begat a further legend: a belief developed that if two in love burned the book and stood together in its smoke, their romance would resist all decay and mellowing.

In his seventies, living in the foothills and limping, with the town integrated, and many of the young marrying without much consequence or stigma across the old breach, Mazzu shook his head with a mixed expression when he contemplated his one beautiful act in life was telling the people of Baraffo a lewd and beguiling lie.

ACKNOWLEDGEMENTS

I would like to graciously acknowledge the Canada Council for the Arts, the Ontario Arts Council, and the Toronto Arts Council for their support.

Stays at the Château de Lavigny Writers' Residence, Saari Artists Residency, and MacDowell gave me dedicated writing time. Thank you to the teams at each of these residencies that sustain these valuable places.

Thank you to Jay and Hazel Millar at Book*hug Press, Peter Norman for his editing insights, and Mikhail Iossel and Alessandro Porco for their helpful suggestions. This work would not have been possible without Carolyn Smart's acumen, belief, and encouragement.

Thank you to Zara, Laiq, and Liz who make each day a joy.

PHOTO: CALVIN THOMAS

ABOUT THE AUTHOR

Moez Surani's writing has been published internationally, including in *Harper's Magazine*, *Best American Experimental Writing 2016*, *Best Canadian Poetry*, and the *Globe and Mail*. He has received a Chalmers Arts Fellowship, which supported research in India and East Africa, and he has been an artist-in-residence in Finland, Italy, Latvia, Myanmar, Switzerland, Taiwan, the Banff Centre for the Arts in Canada, and at MacDowell in the United States. He is the author of four poetry books: *Reticent Bodies* (2009), *Floating Life* (2012), *Operations* (2016), and *Are the Rivers in Your Poems Real* (2019). Surani lives in Toronto.

COLOPHON

Manufactured as the first edition of
The Legend of Baraffo
in the fall of 2023 by Book*hug Press

Edited for the press by Peter Norman
Copy edited by Shannon Whibbs
Proofread by Charlene Chow
Type + design by Ingrid Paulson

Printed in Canada

bookhugpress.ca